by

JENNIFER JANE POPE

CHIMERA

Thyme II Thyme first published in 2002 by
Chimera Publishing Ltd
PO Box 152
Waterlooville
Hants
PO8 9FS

Printed and bound in Great Britain by
Omnia Books Ltd, Glasgow.

THYME II THYME

Jennifer Jane Pope

This novel is fiction – in real life practice safe sex

The men, Hacklebury men especially, were bad enough, Angelina knew, but the maids and the other women were even worse, especially the cruel-eyed Meg, who made no attempt to disguise the way she relished every moment of her master's wife's suffering.

'Strip the hussy to her corset!' Meg snapped. 'Strip her down and then bring her round to the small pond. We'll give her a thorough soaking, and then you two can tighten her laces even more. She still has on the leather corset with the leather laces, I presume?'

'Yes ma'am,' the younger of the two under-maids, Florence, replied eagerly. 'Master said she was to be kept in it other'n either he or you said different. Said there's two more of the same been ordered, so she could be changed if'n she got a bit too sweaty and smelly.'

'Let her sweat and smell,' Meg growled. 'T'won't be long now before he'll not want to roger the bitch any more any ways.'

Author's Preface

It's a funny old world. It always has been and I guess it always will be, at least while there are still people running it, or people who think they're running it. I've just heard announced on the news that scientists are developing an anti-fat pill that will be on sale all over the world by the year two thousand and ten. They don't say how much it will cost, but the thought crosses my mind that we will end up with a class of sleek and slim rich people while the poor people will be split into two types – *fat*, because they cannot afford the pill and cannot stick to a diet, and *thin*, because they cannot afford any sort of diet in the first place. Some things will never change.

But then a lot of things will change, as a lot of things have already. Journeying back to the early Victorian age with our heroine, Teena Thyme, is a sure-fire way of seeing for ourselves just how much has changed in little over a century-and-a-half, and not just in regards to physical circumstances. Psychologically, there have also been many changes, not the least of which is the way women are now largely regarded, more and more as individuals in their own right and by-and-large equal to men except in physical strength. Unlike poor little Angelina, women are no longer mere chattels totally dominated by their fathers and then by their husbands.

But enough of the history lesson, for it is all there for you to discover in the *Teena* books and in libraries full of research volumes and historical novels. Let us concentrate on our little time-traveller instead.

When I first conceived the idea of a girl who was plunged back and forth through the centuries, I knew it would take a very special sort of character, for anything less would surely have led the poor girl into madness and despair. But then, I thought, aren't all of us, potentially at least, 'special' in our individual and very different ways? Whole nations have risen together in deepest adversity and people grow and develop with every challenge they face.

And yet Teena is very much an individual, for I swear I played little part in her creation. True, I did find her a name, and yes, there is the obvious pun in there, but that is where my control ended.

Teena herself sprang off the page – or out of the computer, if you prefer – as bumptious, as irreverent and as feisty as you meet her here and may well, I hope, have met her in the first book, *Teena Thyme*. Maybe it's because she's wealthy enough now not to have to worry what other people might think of her, or maybe there's a spirit in her that has grown through the ages to manifest itself in her personality, but I got the feeling almost from the beginning that our Teena is not a girl to be messed with.

Not that she's nasty, far from it, but there *is* a grit and a determination in our gal that is the stuff from which empires were forged, and held, against impossible odds. There is even something of the air of a female John Wayne about her, mixed possibly with a touch of Katherine Hepburn at her most formidable. Yet she is no silver-screen icon, for Teena, wherever and whenever she goes, is also much like Michael Caine in that she never plays a character

6

but rather assimilates it and lets the character play her.

Teena's sense of humour ranges from the totally black to the almost childishly flippant, but she is never less than honest, not only with the reader and me but also with herself. Whether she is the five-foot-eleven and fit modern-day gal she introduces herself as, or whether she is only five-feet tall and delicate to a painful extreme, she is forever Teena inside, whatever the outside might say.

Because of this I have to admit that of all my characters, heroes, heroines or villains – and I have created a few hundred by now – none give me as much pleasure or satisfaction during the act of writing as does our little Miss Thyme, for she mostly seems to write herself and I just sit here as an amused and interested observer. I seem to have as little control over her actions and reactions as Teena herself does over the fates and perils the whirling cosmos inflicts upon her. But then that's probably just as well, for otherwise would she still be the Teena she undoubtedly is?

The perceived wisdom in the erotica genre has for many years been that you cannot mix sex and humour. I think Teena has proved that perception to be wrong and, whilst I would like to thank my editor, Adrian, for having the courage to allow me let Teena rip, I would also like to thank the thousands of you who have gone out and backed our judgment with your money. I would also like to thank those of you, wherever you might be in the world, who have taken the time to write to me and tell me just how much you enjoyed the first Teena book. To you I would like to say that, yes, there will be more Teena books, beginning with this one. I think there is also a fair chance there will be some graphic adventures and perhaps even an animated film not too far in the future, although strictly speaking, maybe a long way in the past.

For those of you who are meeting Teena for the first time here, I have let her introduce herself again in the following pages – try stopping her – but space prevents even her going on at too great a length. However, there is another option open to those of you with Internet access...

Before the first book was published, we took the very unusual step of releasing a sampler of it on my website, not merely a few hundred words to whet the appetite but the first quarter of the entire novel, more than twenty-thousand words. In those pages you meet Teena properly, learn all about her and get a very good idea of the sorts of adventures and predicaments she blunders into. By the end of the sampler, you have little doubt as to whether you are likely to love or hate her.

Thankfully, sales of *Teena Thyme*, and the critical and fan response, indicate that most of you have fallen under her spell and cannot wait for more. Well, wait no more, unless...

Unless you haven't read that first book, in which case you can either try finding a copy or, at least to begin with, visit my web site at *www.avid-diva.com* and click on the *Books* link to find that extended extract. If you can't find a copy of the book in a shop near you, you might try going to Chimera's website, *www.chimerabooks.co.uk*. You can also go to *amazon.co.uk*, and if you live abroad, you can visit *amazon.com*.

You can find Teena almost anywhere nowadays. But the bigger question is, where will *Teena* find herself next?

Many thanks to you all for your support and enthusiasm, and may you all look forward to a future just a little more certain and a lot less fraught than the past to which our Teena looks back.

And do not forget, Teena's adventures are a work of fiction, so do not try most of this at home! Be safe, be sane, be consensual and be happy. All my love to you,

Jenny Jane Pope

Prologue – Time Travel

Even after more than a quarter of a century doing it, I still
don't know how it works, but then the fact that I also
still don't really understand how a couple of manmade
wings can lift a jumbo jet to the upper reaches of the
atmosphere doesn't mean *that* doesn't happen. Just take
my word for it – jumbo jets fly and people *can* travel
through time. I'm not the only one who does it, I'm just
one of the very few people prepared to talk about it, let
alone write it all down like this.

The few really close friends with whom I've discussed
my various adventures, and whose encouragements
finally led me to begin documenting them, have expressed
a certain… well, I'm not quite sure what the best words
are to describe what they say, but they all tend to wonder
how and why it is that wherever I turn up through the
ages it tends to be in the midst of a bunch of what I
politely describe as perverted lunatics. Again, politeness
not withstanding, I know that my friends – being aware
that most, if not all, of the bodies I find myself in are in
some way physically related to the 'me' of the twenty-
first century – must also be wondering as to my own,
shall we say, stability.

Well, for those of you similarly disposed, let me assure
you that I'm as stable as the next girl and more stable
than most. If I have a propensity for enduring the bizarre
without going to pieces, and questioning the morality of

minds and bodies that can derive a certain amount of gratification from situations many might describe as less than so-called normal, so what? I didn't ask to be thrown back and forth like this, and until my very first adventure I had no real idea of the sort of kinks that exist within so many people.

Given the choice between being swept off my feet by a modern day Mister Darcy, all champagne and chocolates and just a hint of dark brooding to keep me on my toes, and being harnessed up like a race horse and having the arse screwed off me whilst champing on a foul tasting gag, then the chocolates and champagne would win every time. But it's not even a case of beggars not being choosers we're talking about here. Believe me, I've begged, been made to beg, crawling on all fours with an artificial tail plugged into my bottom for added effect and humiliation, and I can tell you that begging never did me any good whatsoever.

No, my philosophy, if you can call it that, has been very simple from the start – don't beat yourself up over something you can't do anything about. And, given the opportunity, take the best out of everything going, even if the best means surrendering yourself to the treacherous leanings of whatever body you happen to find yourself in, and of whatever situation that body itself happens to be in.

I guess you probably think that makes me some sort of kink? Well, okay, I suppose you probably have a point there. Yes, maybe it does, but then perhaps you're also confusing me with someone else, someone who gives a flying fuck, perhaps? Don't knock what you haven't tried, and don't even think of sitting in judgment on me or anyone else who might be out there like me. Being plucked from the present and sent back through the centuries at random intervals and without so much as a second's warning is more than enough for us to have to worry about. Besides, as I've already said, why should I get all moral about bodies that aren't my own?

It's my lot, that's all, and I can't fight it, so I go with the flow and, if I were really brutally honest, I'd have to say that it hasn't been *all* bad. I've seen things, been places and met people I know many of my contemporaries would give their eye teeth to have seen, been and met, and I've learned stuff about history you almost certainly won't find in any history books, at least not in the history books you get in schools and public libraries.

And then there's the other up side to all this, which are my own body and my own life in the here and now. Yes, *this* body, that's the one I'm talking about, the tall one with the very long legs, nice firm breasts and, even if I do say so myself, not unattractive face, a twenty-something girl's face, in fact. It comes as just a bit of a shock to most people when I tell them that it's more than a passable face for someone who's knocking on the door to join the *Over Fifty's Club*.

Yes, it's true, but as I explained in the first volume of my little memoir, it's some sort of side effect of time-travel and I can't explain how it works any better than I can explain the rest of it. No, that's not true, I can explain *how* it works but not *why*, at least in basic mathematics. For every minute, hour, day, or whatever span of time that I spend back in some other age, my body in the present gets awarded some sort of credit to the equivalent. In other words, if I go back into the past for a week, then

12

for the next week that I'm back in my own time my real body won't age.

And that's a better deal than it might sound at first hearing, because when I say I go back in time for a week, that week is seven days in time *then* but only a matter of seconds in the present, or in real time. In any one week of my own time, I could spend maybe as much as several months back in the past and thereby have earned myself half a year or more of non-aging in the process. At least that's the way it seems to work. If I'm right, I've now racked up a credit of around five or six years that I haven't even touched yet. So even if, for whatever reason, my time hopping adventures were to stop tomorrow, it would be another five or six years before my body, which I think of as my real body, started back onto the normal process of deterioration.

I hope.

As explanations go, the above may not rank in the Top Twenty, but it's about as good as it gets when it comes from me, so maybe it would be better to leave it as it stands and get back to my story.

You do remember my story, don't you?

Okay, it's been a while, so I won't hold it against you if you don't, and there'll be people out there reading this who may well have missed out on my first tome, so let's just refresh ourselves, shall we?

I'm Teena Thyme, eponymous heroine, as they would have it, of the book *Teena Thyme* and now of this book, which we have wittily entitled *Thyme II Thyme*. To be really accurate, I'm actually Christeena Felicity Spigwell-Thyme, but the grand sounding name doesn't make for a grand pedigree, at least not through the most immediate

13

layers and branches of my family tree. Christeena I got because my dad is dyslexic and was drunk when he went to register my birth, and Felicity was from my late grandmother. I'm just grateful that dad somehow got Felicity right even if he screwed up on spelling what was supposed to be Christina, otherwise the gods alone know what combinations I might have ended up with.

Spigwell-Thyme being a bit of a mouthful, my parents had tended to drop the first bit and stick with good old-fashioned Thyme, as in sage, rosemary, etc. I'm also grateful that the brilliant idea my dad had to call me Rosemary was given a very firm knock on the head by the rest of the family. A joke is a joke and a pun is a pun, but Rosemary Thyme? I don't think so!

Anyway, where was I? Ah yes, well, we weren't a very posh family. Dad had a well enough paid job as an engineer in sewage, and mum was a part-time teacher in the local infant's school right up to the day when they closed it and merged it with a bigger place about six miles up the road. Home for wee Teena was a modest house at a place called Sandy Point on Hayling Island, which for the uninitiated is a lump of land sticking out of the south coast just slightly to the east of Portsmouth, in Hampshire.

I won't bore you with any more geographical details here. If you want to find out for yourself, get an AA road map and look it up. On second thought, spare yourself the expense and effort, it isn't worth it, believe me.

Life for me up until I reached my majority, as they call it, was pretty much uneventful, just the usual kid stuff, going to the usual schools and doing the usual things. Much like your own early years, I suspect, so we'll gloss over those and move forward to when I turned eighteen, by which time the most remarkable things about me were that I had grown to the unusual height, for a girl, of five-feet-eleven. Because I was fit and strong in addition to being tall, I had represented my school and county at netball and had half-a-dozen silver-plated trophies along with a drawer full of silver-plated medals to prove it. I might not be proud of a lot of things I've done in my life, but at least I can be proud of that.

But I digress...

My birthday is the eighteenth of December, precisely one week before Christmas. When my eighteenth birthday arrived, late in nineteen seventy-four, it was accompanied by a letter from a firm of lawyers in relatively nearby Chichester asking me to present myself at their offices, whereupon I would learn something to my advantage. They weren't kidding.

It turned out I'd had a great aunt, maybe with a few extra 'greats' thrown in for good measure, a Miss Amelia Spigwell, who had just died, but not before living to the age of one-hundred-and-three. She had never married, as her one true love had been killed in the Boer War, and none of us Spigwell-Thymes had ever been aware of her existence even though she had lived in a small cottage in a village called Rowland's Castle only a hop, skip and a jump from Hayling Island.

We'd also had no idea, therefore, that she had been quite rich, so it came as a bit of a surprise to one eighteen-year-old Teena to discover that she was the sole heiress to an estate worth nearly half a million quid, and this back in early nineteen seventy-five, when half a million went a hell of a lot farther than it does today.

To cut a long story short, I moved into the cottage to

do the independent miss bit, though I was determined to continue with my studies. In particular I was into history, but was totally unprepared for just *how* into history I was to become. I had barely time to consider my newfound wealth when I stumbled over several old trunks and cases left by, I presumed, the late Amelia. Well, stumbled over isn't exactly accurate as they were up with the spiders' webs in the loft, but I did find them. They seemed to be mostly full of old clothes, dresses, underwear, shoes, boots and even some costume jewellery all dating back at least seventy years and possibly even further. None of it was valuable, other than possibly attracting a few quid from memorabilia collectors, but it was all in remarkably good condition, nearly new, in fact, presumably because the trunks were all but airtight.

Now, you show me a girl who isn't attracted by a heap of glamorous gowns and who doesn't have just a teensy hankering for days when ladies were ladies and men were men – or rakes, or cads, or whatever – and I'll show you a girl who's either a liar or who doesn't have a scrap of romanticism or imagination in her body. Hot pants and miniskirts may have been considered sexy back in the sixties and seventies, but silk and taffeta are the stuff of dreams…

Corsets, on the other hand, are the stuff of nightmares, whatever they may do for your figure, and wouldn't you just know it, there was no way I was going to get any of those dresses hooked or buttoned without first submitting myself to the tortures of the boned underwear selection I found with them. So I huffed and I puffed and I damn nearly passed out, but eventually down the stairs came one Lady Teena, all rustle and bustle, high-heels and long gloves, heading straight for the medicinal properties of a bottle of wine.

Which was when I discovered the pendant, hidden away, probably lost, in a dark recess in the kitchen. It was a locket, and inside was a miniature of a lady and a gentleman, a nice and very proper looking pair, vintage Georgian or early Victorian. There was nothing special about them and nothing special about the pendant either, I thought, other than the fact it was most definitely gold. How wrong could I have been?

I have since discovered that the pendant, thought not *de rigeur* for my time hopping, almost certainly was the initial catalyst. Exactly what it triggered in me and in the cosmos I have no idea, but trigger something it most certainly did.

I put the pendant on.

I fainted.

I woke up back in eighteen thirty-nine and, more to the point, I woke up in a corset even tighter than the one I had just struggled into and in a body that was most definitely not my own. I knew this for a fact because, other than being blonde like me, this girl had been barely five-feet tall in her stocking feet and had breasts you could have fit into one fair sized hand as a pair. I may not have been overly endowed but I had more up top than that!

Her name, it transpired, was Angelina and she was an ancestor, but that bit was less important than the fact that she was about to be forced into marriage with a particularly nasty piece of work called Sir Gregory Hacklebury, and that she was being held prisoner by a man to whom being called a bounder would have been a compliment. His chief maid, a demented female called Meg who was undoubtedly shagging his lights out, had been put in charge of the poor wench and was delighting in taunting and torturing her at every tip and turn.

Of course, it was all about money; Gregory had little and Angelina had lots, and in those days when a woman married a man everything she had became his property, including her body. Oh dear, what a shock to a modern lass like myself.

The rest I'll fill you in on as we go, but for the moment I should also add that when I finally returned to my own body and my own time, I met up with and befriended a girl slightly older than myself called Anne-Marie. I should also mention that she had several cousins by the name of Hacklebury who came from in and around a little village called Melbury Osmand in the neighbouring county of Dorset. She also had a sort of stepbrother named Andy, although Andy, it transpired, preferred to dress and act more like an Andrea, except when it came to exercising his little Percy department. I suppose you would call Anne-Marie bi-sexual and you would call Andy... well, you would call him unusual, at the very least. The same could be said of Anne-Marie, for she quickly introduced me to a combination of lesbian sex and bondage games, although not bondage in the true and cruel sense I'd experienced more than a century earlier.

We did a bit of research together. I had carefully explained what had happened to me to Anne-Marie and, wonder of wonders, she believed me and we went and met her cousins under some pretext or other. However, whilst there was a sort of Hacklebury resemblance in some of them, especially bachelor cousin George, there was nothing conclusive other than that we returned from

Dorset with the certainty in our minds that Hacklebury must have fathered a child with Angelina, and that the line had continued. As to where that line had led and what direct or indirect links it had with me in the present, I had no idea. And to be honest, as the psychological scars began to heal quickly, I resolved to drop the whole thing once and for all and forget the past. Unfortunately, the 'thing' refused to drop me. Right in the middle of Andrea giving me the screwing of all time, I was whisked back once more...

Chapter One

'Jeez, Teenie, you had us both really worried there for a couple of minutes!'

Anne-Marie's voice penetrated the mists and I forced my eyes to open. I saw their two faces, Anne-Marie's to my right, Andrea's to my left, consternation on the former, sheer fright on the latter.

'No, don't try to get up.' Anne-Marie pressed gently against my shoulders. 'Take it easy... there's a love. You passed out, in case you didn't guess already, and you look terrible.' She stroked my forehead and I realised the gag and harness were gone, as was the ribbon that had bound my wrists earlier, though my hands were still encased within the disabling gloves.

'Here,' Andrea said, turning away, 'try a sip of water.' Her hand hovered back into my field of vision and I saw she was holding a half filled glass.

I shook my head, but Anne-Marie already had her arm beneath my shoulders, lifting me and steadying me. I sipped indelicately; the cold liquid spilled out onto my chin but I didn't care.

'Better?' Andrea asked gently.

I nodded, grateful when I was allowed to fall back and sink into the softness of the pillow Anne-Marie had pulled beneath me with her free hand.

'A bit too much too soon, I think,' she said soberly.

I looked up into her eyes and shook my head again.

'No,' I managed to say, my voice half croak, half whisper. 'No, it was quite…' Mere words could not have gone even halfway down the road to describing what I had felt, but it was more than that, and something else, that I had to tell them. 'It was good,' I said lamely. 'Better than good, but…' I hesitated, once more at a loss for words. 'How long was I out for this time?' I asked instead.

I saw Anne-Marie's expression changing as understanding dawned in her eyes. 'Oh, my God!' she exclaimed, her hand rising to her mouth. 'You mean you went back there again?'

I heard a half strangled gasp from Andrea but my attention was now fixed firmly on Anne-Marie. 'Yes,' I said, 'I went back there again. How long have I been unconscious?'

Anne-Marie's mouth puckered and she looked across at Andrea. 'Five minutes,' she said. 'Maybe six, no longer than that.'

'No,' Andrea agreed, 'not long, though we were both really worried about you.'

'Sorry,' I said stupidly. Now I did try to sit up. Aided by Anne-Marie, I managed it, and then held my head in my near-useless hands breathing as deeply as the tight corset would permit. 'Five or six minutes, you say? And I definitely never left here at all during that time?'

'Of course you didn't,' Anne-Marie replied firmly. 'We lifted you onto the bed and untied everything and then I was slapping your face and splashing water on you, though nothing seemed to have any effect. I was on the point of calling an ambulance, but then suddenly you started to come around again.'

'Good job I did.' Despite everything I had just been

through, I chuckled imagining the expressions on the faces of the paramedics called in to revive me in my present get-up. Then I sighed and lowered my hands. 'It didn't feel like a dream,' I told them quietly, looking up at the two pairs of eyes fixed immovably on me. 'It felt dead real again. Too damned real, actually.' My hand went up to touch the locket that still hung around my neck and my fingers stroked the smooth metal of the casing. Idly, I noticed they had removed the choker I'd been wearing around my neck earlier. 'And it was far longer than five minutes, believe me,' I went on. 'More like five weeks, at a guess.' I drew in another deep breath and shook my head. 'I need a stiff drink,' I announced. 'A bloody big stiff drink!'

'But what about—?' Anne-Marie stopped herself.

I smiled up at her. 'A drink first,' I said fervently. 'A drink first, and then I'll tell you all about it, though trust me, you aren't going to believe me.'

'Go get her a large brandy, Andrea,' she commanded.

I laughed. 'Bring the bottle and three glasses, and a spare one if you've got one – a spare bottle, that is. This is some story, and you're both going to need a drink almost as much as I am!'

The men, Hacklebury men especially, were bad enough, Angelina knew, but the maids and the other women were even worse, especially the cruel-eyed Meg, who made no attempt to disguise the way she relished every moment of her master's wife's suffering.

'Strip the hussy to her corset!' Meg snapped. 'Strip her down and then bring her round to the small pond. We'll give her a thorough soaking, and then you two can tighten

her laces even more. She still has on the leather corset with the leather laces, I presume?'

'Yes ma'am,' the younger of the two under-maids, Florence, replied eagerly. 'Master said she was to be kept in it other'n either he or you said different. Said there's two more of the same been ordered, so she could be changed if'n she got a bit too sweaty and smelly.'

'Let her sweat and smell,' Meg growled. 'T'won't be long now before he'll not want to roger the bitch any more any ways.'

'Can't see what he finds attractive in her meself,' the second under-maid said, and giggled. She was older than Florence, though younger by some few years than Meg herself, and had about her the look of one who had been brought up in the fresh country air. She preened herself and thrust her chest forward so that her substantial bosom strained against the black linen of her uniform.

'She ain't ever going to have teats like yours, Betty, that's for sure,' Florence said with admiration. 'Skinny as a bloody garden rake, she is. More meat on a butcher's apron, as my old pa would say,' she added cheerfully as she drew the top of the bodice down about Angelina's arms, revealing her small breasts thrust cruelly upwards by the strictures of her tightly laced undergarment.

'Not even a decent mouthful there.' Betty sniffed disdainfully and reached out one finger to trace a line gently across the small mounds where they emerged from the lacy top ruff of the corset. 'Maybe we should give a little suck every day and see if we can't maybe encourage the little eggs to grow.'

'You can suck her tits any time you like,' Meg declared, 'but it won't make the buggers grow any more. That's an *old wives' tale, that is. Only thing'll make those titties get bigger is if'n either his lordship or one of his kind plants a sprig in her, which'll like as not happen soon enough, if'n it hasn't happened already.'*

'Little belly's going to be full of arms and legs?' Florence rubbed an open palm across Angelina's flat stomach. 'Well, at least it'll get you a bit of relief from all these stays.' She laughed again and patted the whalebone-encased figure in a manner that under different circumstances might have been interpreted as friendly or sympathetic.

But Angelina knew only too well that these horrific people had no such emotions to spare where she was concerned. 'Damn you!' she said. 'Damn all of you! Damn all of you to hell!'

Florence stepped back and sneered down at her, her florid face contorted into an expression of contempt. 'And fuck you, little mistress,' she hissed, 'because that's just what he's going to do, you know. He's going to fuck you until that pretty little fanny is red raw and that oh-so-trim little belly grows round and fat.'

'Yes, you little cow,' Betty snickered, 'and then we'll be here to see you properly milked every day, won't we, Flo?'

'That we will,' Florence agreed. 'We'll make sure the little calf sucks good and hard on those dugs, that we will.'

'That's enough!' Meg snapped, stepping forward. She stretched out a hand and stroked the side of Angelina's face. 'Our little cow will come to discover the truth soon enough, but meanwhile let's just try to help her come to terms with her role, shall we?' She stood back again, pursing her lips and nodding. 'He only wants you for

breeding, you know that, don't you? And it doesn't really even matter which cock does the necessary, either. Just so long as someone plants the sprig, that's all it takes, and then we'll see what the future holds. For myself, my dear little mistress,' she continued, leaning close to Angelina, 'I just cannot wait!'

Even before I opened my eyes I knew I was back, back in eighteen thirty-nine, that is, and also back in big trouble, for I could smell that mixture of my own perspiration and the tight leather into which I had been laced, and my hips and arse throbbed from having lain too long in the straw on the hard floor of my specially built prison.

I struggled into a sitting position, no mean feat without the use of my hands, which were still trapped inside those awful disabling gloves, my wrists locked to the broad corset belt that was part of the suit. Then, grunting into the foul tasting leather gag that was strapped between my achingly distended jaws, I managed to stand up using the rough stone wall as support. Just as before, my feet were encased in those ridiculously high heels and I had to pause for a moment to re-accustom myself and balance before finally tottering across to where the top half of the stable door stood open, the bottom half locked and bolted against any hope of escape.

My field of vision hampered by the narrow eye slits in the all-encompassing tight leather hood I wore, I peered out to where the outer door of my prison stood wide open. No sign of my huge Viking minder as yet, though there was little doubt in my mind that friend Erik was not far away.

The first fingers of dawn were beginning to stretch

against the dark sky in the east…

Like hell they were. In reality, the sky was a very dark grey with just a hint of the deep navy blue tinge that lets you know it's no longer actually night but that it will be another twenty minutes at least before it will be light enough to see anything, and that the chance of the morning sun coming up within the hour has been made more than unlikely by a thick layer of clouds.

I sniffed at the air, mostly a waste of time and effort really as the leather smell of my mask was all-pervasive, but I did get enough from that whiff to know it was damp outside and therefore not much better inside. The tight kid bodysuit they were keeping me in was less than comfortable, but at least it offered some protection, both against the elements and against my chafing or grazing myself on unsympathetic surfaces.

Yet was that the main reason for strapping and lacing me into this accursed garment? The main reason possibly, but not the sole reason. Hacklebury had some very curious ideas when it came to women and what he considered sexy, and figure-hugging leather fell into that category. What was it with men and leather? The magazines I'd seen, both behind the bushes at the edge of the school playing field and on the top shelves of a couple of newsagent's shops in Havant and Portsmouth, featured shiny black-clad female figures in outfits ranging from the more conventional motorcycle jacket and trousers – the jacket usually open in front to reveal varying degrees of amazingly well-developed mammary glands – to corsets I had regarded as being impossibly constricting, up until I'd been introduced to the real thing, that is.

I turned back from the doorway and stared at the

featureless walls, pondering glumly. No, this whole thing smacked of something even deeper than Hacklebury being a leather fetishist. His mad maidservant had a hand in everything, or so it seemed, and apparently she was able to exercise an influence over her employer far above her presumed station as a mere domestic. She was obviously sane enough to appreciate that the likes of dear Gregory could never marry the likes of her, but she was determined to make it clear to me that my situation as his wife was considered even lower than her own might have been, even had I actually been his wife.

My thoughts turned to whoever it was they had found and used as my doppelganger, the girl who had stood in at the travesty of a wedding ceremony to make sure Angelina didn't say 'I won't' when it came time to say 'I do'. I still didn't know much about my ancestor, who's dainty little body I now once again occupied, but there was a feeling I couldn't get away from that she had a courage far greater than most young women of her age would have possessed. She had stood up to Hacklebury and to Meg and that was no mean effort, for she must have known the awful pair would make her pay for her defiance.

Where are you now, Angelina? I wondered, and grimaced in a kind of smile around the disfiguring gag. Her body was here, of course, and I was in it, but where was her actual spirit, her so-called soul? Was she still in here with me somewhere, dormant, or simply keeping a low profile while I took over? Or was she elsewhere, maybe in someone else's body or simply floating in the ether? Could she see me? Could she feel me? Did she know I existed? Was she watching me now, perhaps even tuning into my thoughts?

Talk to me, you silly little bitch!

No answer. I waited, listening both outwardly and inwardly.

I could do with your help, Angelina. You may have a few answers that could be a bit useful.

Still nothing.

I'm on your side, girl, and two heads are better than one. Of course, in our case, it was a matter of only one head between us and maybe two minds, but I'm sure you get the idea, and I hoped and assumed she would, too, if only she was listening.

Please? Pretty please?

I sighed. Oh well, I hadn't really expected her to suddenly pop up on the side. She'd made no effort to communicate the first time I'd found myself in her body, so why would she bother now? The conclusion, therefore, had to be that she couldn't rather than *wouldn't* communicate with me.

You're on your own, Teena my girl. How long this time, I wondered, trying to remember exactly how long the experience had lasted the first time. It had seemed like an eternity while I was going through it, but it had probably only been a few days, while back in the year nineteen seventy-five it had only been a few minutes. My eyes narrowed as I thought of Anne-Marie and Andrea. Presumably, I would have passed out in front of them and they would be doing their best to revive me, Andrea possibly thinking I had fainted as a result of her efforts with her otherwise carefully disguised manhood.

I felt guilty as sin when I thought about how little persuasion it had taken for me to fit in with my odd new

28

friends' weird sexual proclivities, and because straps and chains hadn't really been needed in order for Anne-Marie to reduce me to a kneeling little slave with my tongue licking eagerly at her dripping pussy. I stared down at myself as best I could, and a shiver of something ran up my spine. I tried not to admit to what had caused it, but deep inside me I damn well knew the truth.

The games I had played with Anne-Marie and Andrea were just that, games. They had been exciting, but this now was no game and these chains, though not actually any more real than Anne-Marie's, had been locked onto me with an intent approaching permanence. No, this was no dalliance or role-playing but a game that was being enacted in deadly earnest, and this bondage was both thorough and cruel, designed to reduce me to the level of a helpless plaything with a status scarcely above that of any four legged stable inmate…

And that thought excited me, I realised with horror!

As the leather corset began to dry out, its laces started shrinking and tightening even more despite the fact that Angelina had been convinced the last round of tightening, following her dunking into the pond, had constricted her waist as far as was humanly possible.

The two younger maids had earlier bound her wrists with another length of lace, although this they had used dry and not allowed to become wet afterwards. However, the various turns were tight enough and cinched through so that Angelina knew there was no chance of her slipping out of this simple bondage. Now she was helpless to try and ease her newest torture even had her fingers been able to deal with the knots that held the corset closed. All she could do was stand and try to stare back at the three women with an air of defiance, a posture and attitude made increasingly difficult, and eventually impossible, as the unforgiving garment drew tighter and tighter about her.

Finally, with a gasp and a small squeal, she sank to her knees. 'Mercy!' she cried, blinking away tears of pain and humiliation. 'Mercy, I beg of you, before you kill me!'

Meg stepped forward, stooped over her and seized her hair, hauling her head up so Angelina was forced to look into her sneering face. 'Oh, you'll not die, you simpering child,' she said quietly. 'You may faint, and you'll fight for every breath, but you'll not die, not for a long while yet, I promise you.'

Angelina groaned, her eyes wide and her nostrils dilated as the air hissed in and out of her protesting lungs. 'And then what?' she begged to know, the words now little more than a series of sobs. 'What is it you want of me?'

'Want? Of you? Ha!' Meg released her vicious grip and allowed the blonde head to drop forward again. 'I want nothing of you, little missy,' she said in a tone of dismissive contempt. 'The master did want certain things, but you have made it obvious you cannot, or will not, provide them, more fool you, and now it is simply a case of teaching you how to behave.' She turned to the other maids. 'Go, both of you,' she ordered. 'Get back to the house and prepare the horse. I'll bring this creature with me shortly.'

The two maids scuttled off in a swirl of skirts and petticoats, leaving Meg alone with Angelina. The older woman now crouched down beside her captive and raised her chin in one hand. 'I'll have everything I want, miss cold fish,' she hissed. 'I already have most of it, in fact, and when you are no longer of any use or value, I shall have it completely.'

'You want Gregory for yourself?' Angelina whimpered.

Meg laughed. 'I already have him, in truth, and now I also have you, and by his order, whilst it makes my flesh creep to think of him with his proud cock in such a tight and unresponsive pussy as yours, by God I shall turn you into his whore as well as his wife.'

'But why? Surely that will go against your hopes if I were to do all the wicked things I know he wants of me?'

'Then you do not know men, little girl,' Meg retorted. 'When you are finally ready and are begging him for it, lapping his cock and balls at every tip and turn and squirming like a three penny slut at his feet, what appeal do you think you will have for him then? You, with your tiny titties and skinny shanks, do you think a man like that will choose you over what I offer him? Ah, I know he can never marry me nor give me his name in any way, but have him I shall in every other fashion.'

'And then you will kill me, I suppose?' Angelina fought to get the words out as the pressure around her diaphragm continued to intensify.

Meg patted her cheek. 'Perhaps, in time,' she conceded, 'but first I'll have you as my little lap dog, madam. You'll crawl to me as you would crawl to him and offer me that tart little tongue as readily as I will accept it where it belongs, down here!' She jerked a finger towards her skirts. 'Yes, down here, my little bitch, your little tongue will lap my pussy to prepare it for your very own husband, and then you will watch as he rogers a real woman.'

'You're mad!' Angelina groaned, her eyes widening in even greater horror. 'I... I thought Gregory was mad enough, but... but you... you are completely... insane!' The last word emerged as a strangled squeal and faded into a sigh as she toppled forward, fainting into merciful oblivion.

Memories or dreams? Dreams or memories? *Her* memories or *my* dreams? As I opened my eyes to find myself once again staring at the blank stone walls of my confinement, I knew I had already begun to understand and accept the truth.

Wherever Angelina's own personality now was, little snippets of her memories were beginning to filter through to me. It started happening the last time I had come back, and now... still like a half remembered dream after waking but clearer, much clearer than before. Or was it, had it been, simply my imagination?

I turned slowly, studying each of the walls in turn trying to use their very blankness to focus and concentrate my mind. The scene by the pond had been real, of that I was all but certain, and now as I narrowed my eyes I found I could almost relive it, the vice-like pressure of that awful corset, the sharp pains against my spine as the steadily shrinking laces cut into my flesh... no, not *my* flesh, *her* flesh.

I shook my head, blinking fiercely. Her flesh, my flesh, what did it matter? This was her body, but now it was my body again. And for how long?

A terrible thought struck me and my teeth dug deeper into the leather gag. How long before the murderous bitch finally tired of her game and killed her helpless victim?

And what if that helpless victim just still happened to be me at the time? Would I die in, and with, this body? Reason told me that I ought not to; that if I was Angelina when the time came I would simply be whisked back to my own time and body. But reason had played no part in this so far, so why should it begin to now or any time in the future?

I shuddered and the sound of my heart pounding grew louder still in my head, so loud I did not hear the footsteps approaching from beyond the stable door…

To say that the jailer Hacklebury had appointed for me was a big man would not be doing his size justice in any way, shape or form; Erik was huge. I would have found his height and bulk intimidating even in my real body, so imagine how much more terrifying and powerful he seemed to me trapped in Angelina's tiny five-foot frame.

There was something about him that said 'Viking' to me and indeed, I quickly discovered that he was Scandinavian, though I was never totally certain which of those northern countries he actually came from, perhaps it was a mixture of more than one. He spoke very clear English and so was able to communicate his instructions and requirements, if one did not count the peculiar backwards way he had of constructing his sentences, which after a surprisingly short time I came to cope with quite easily. Blond and bulky with muscles, Erik was also more than passably good looking, to the point of even being handsome to women who go for that certain ruggedness. And the fact that he was soft- spoken and prone to smiling a lot sometimes almost made me forget what he was there for, almost but not quite, for he was as ruthlessly efficient in the execution of his duties as he was casual in his handling of me.

Today, it seemed, was to be no different...

'Forward please, and over the rail to be bending.' Erik pointed to the crude trestle arrangement that stood in the centre of the stable cell adjacent to the one in which I was generally kept. Obediently, I shuffled towards it and lowered the upper half of my body over the waist-high horizontal rail. My nemesis quickly moved in and buckled the thick strap across the small of my back, preventing me from rising again until it was released. My arms were now quickly folded behind my back and secured there by means of heavy leather cuffs, and then my ankles were dragged wider apart and similarly fettered. Yet Erik had only just begun.

Behind me, I heard a rattling sound as he sorted through an assortment of bamboo and rattan canes lining a rack in the corner. It seemed that little, if anything, had changed during my short respite back in the twentieth century. I was to be beaten on a regular basis and, even though my buttocks had the questionable luxury of the tight leather for protection, I knew it was still going to hurt, especially when Erik began to trickle water onto my thin and tightly stretched hide. I felt his massive hands massaging the liquid in, and then bit into my gag in frustration when I felt his caresses fire off those all too familiar little crackerjacks of desire deep inside me. *Damn this body!* I thought.

The cane cut through the air and landed precisely in the middle of my left cheek. I squealed through my gagged lips like a piglet, unprepared for that initial scythe of fire despite the fact that I had been both caned and whipped during my previous incarnation here. The addition of the water treatment had a far greater effect on my punishment than I had anticipated.

'Six we shall be having and no more for now,' Erik crooned from somewhere behind me to my left.

Six strokes… well, it could have been far worse, I supposed, but any feeling of relief was instantly thrust aside as the cane hissed down again and delivered a matching cut to my other buttock. I yelped and bucked and only the fact that the trestle was bolted firmly into the floor prevented me from lifting it into the air despite its solid weight. Tears misted my vision and I whimpered and chewed desperately on the gag. Four more strokes to endure and already I felt as if my arse was on fire. Worse still, other more insidious embers of feeling were beginning to fan back into life and I knew that, pain or no pain, by the time Erik put aside his first weapon and began concentrating on his second, I would be hot and wet between my thighs and apparently eager for a cock that was built in proportion to the rest of him.

Swish and *crack! Swish* and *crack!* Two more strokes arrived at evenly spaced and unhurried intervals, each one landing just a finger's breadth below the first. I tried to scream but the gag made it impossible.

'Good it is that from inside your frustrations now relieving you are,' Erik all but sang.

I felt his hand exploring between my legs, probing between the laces that held the crotch opening of my suit together. I groaned again but this time more from embarrassment than pain, for not only did his finger probe easily through one of the gaps, it slid into me with no resistance whatsoever. I heard him grunt with what I presumed was satisfaction, and then the invading digit was withdrawn.

There was a pause, during which I closed my eyes and prayed desperately that he would quickly resume and complete my flogging, for I remembered Meg had promised me there would be variations on the main punishment theme, one of which was that I could expect to be whipped on my breasts. To my immense relief, however, this tactic was not on Erik's mind, at least not on this occasion, and the remaining two cuts duly arrived half an inch or so above the first pair. Then I dimly heard the rattle of the cane being dropped back in the rack, and blinked furiously to clear my vision.

I felt fingers again, this time pulling at the crotch laces, untying them and withdrawing them. I felt more cool air against my vulva, but I could also now feel the warm trickle of my juices across the flesh at the tops of my thighs. It still seemed unbelievable to me that this body, or any other body for that matter, could react in such a fashion. Every nerve fibre was stretched and throbbing with the anguish of the six strokes from the cane, and yet here I was going into full flood with my pussy throbbing for an entirely different reason.

'Good this is, you see?'

I realised that Erik was now standing in front of me and slowly raised my head as far as I could. I was not surprised to see that he had unfastened the front of his own leather breeches and that his manhood was now standing upright in all its undeniable glory. He moved forward, reaching down to unfasten the strap holding the leather gag that was now a sodden mass inside my mouth. And as he withdrew the foul stopper, offering me instead his own crown as a substitute, I knew that ordinarily I should have used my teeth and ensured he would be in no fit state to continue. However, it was as if some remote controller was ruling my temporary body as my lips dutifully parted to suck him in, stretching and distorting in order to accommodate the thick girth of his shaft. Fortunately, for I would surely have choked or suffocated had he continued for any length of time, Erik was content for me to simply lubricate him, though the heavens knew I was already well enough lubricated myself. After allowing me to suck him as far as the back of my throat two or three times, he withdrew his erection and patted the top of my leather-covered head.

'Good girl,' he said in a tone he might have used to commend a pet dog and moved quickly behind me again.

A second or so later, I felt his hard knob pressing between my nether lips and the sensation sent a lurching feeling through my stomach. Another second or so and he was in me, my sodden vagina stretching to accept him with unbelievable ease even though his length and width, once he was fully sheathed inside me and his heavy balls pressed hard against me, gave me the feeling of being completely stuffed.

'Ah,' he sighed, 'good this is, and now fucked you truly shall be,' he promised me.

I barely managed to suppress a sigh of my own for I knew he was quite capable of performing for a long time without reaching a climax whilst I, or Angelina, would begin to lose control at any moment. Sure enough, almost as soon as he began his languid piston-like motion, I found myself writhing in my bonds and attempting to thrust back to meet his advances, moaning each time he filled me again. Stars began to appear behind my closed eyelids, tiny exploding flashes of purple, green and white. Though I ground my teeth together in an effort to resist the pleasure, it was futile and the outcome inevitable.

It wasn't long before I heard myself screaming, not from the fire in my beaten buttocks every time his hard body crashed against them, but from the waves of insatiable desire and ecstasy that possessed me. Indeed, the pain was now absorbed into part of something else and the needling sensation merged with the heat of something I knew should have shamed me totally, were I still capable of feeling such an emotion, which I clearly was not, at least not at the moment.

'Oh, *yes!*' I heard a voice echoing shrilly against the hard walls. As I dimly realised it was me who had shrieked out that barely human cry of exultation, the last of my resistance melted. 'Yes, you great bastard! Yes! Fuck me all you want, I… oh… oh!' What I wanted was obvious enough but I never voiced it for the words disintegrated into moans and groans, gasps and cries. I would hate myself for my capitulation later, but for the moment I cared for nothing more than the massive flesh-and-blood piston within my hot cylinder and the first of the many orgasms towards which it was inexorably driving me.

Strapped down over that trestle there was little else I could have done than surrender my tenanted body to the inevitable, but what followed was far less easy to account for. I can only suggest that in some way my mind had got 'moved' and events seemed to be taking place in that state we all sometimes experience in which they seem to be happening to someone else and we are merely observing them through a slightly smudged or smoky glass.

When Erik finally erupted inside me – and there was no doubting the moment even though I was away on my own planet by then – it was not quite the end of his efforts. He continued pumping away at me for probably another two to three minutes before I felt him gradually begin softening inside me. I should have been overjoyed or at least relieved, but despite the fact that I seemed to have spent half a lifetime writhing like a worm on the end of his hook, I experienced a wave of utter disappointment. When he withdrew from me completely and stepped back, I felt utterly empty and I don't just mean physically; I was absolutely desolate.

For his part, Erik seemed surprisingly drained by his efforts. I say 'surprisingly' because in my earlier encounters with the giant Viking he had always seemed inexhaustible. He released me from the backbreaking restraint, hooked a short leash to my collar and led me across to the far wall, where he slid down onto the straw with the rough stones at his back. Without being told, like an obedient dog, I sat down in front of him and, eyeing his tumescence still on display through the opening in his breeches, I slid myself close to him, extending one hand to take hold of it in my gloved fist.

I should explain here for new readers that apart from being tightly laced and buckled into leather mitts that reached up to become one with the sleeves of the horrible leather bodysuit I was wearing, my hands were also still inside the long gloves Meg had placed on me from the beginning, gloves that looked to be all style and elegance with one slight but important modification. The fingers of these satin niceties were all sewn together, with the thumb likewise sewn to the side of the glove and the lower part of the forefinger. Thus, with or without the mitts, my hands were close to being useless, at least where the performance of any particularly dexterous task was concerned. The double layer removed most of the sensitivity from all my digits, yet I thought I could feel Erik's dozing phallus as I gently began to manipulate it.

Through half closed eyes, he gazed down at my upturned face and smiled contentedly. 'Good it is that sweet you are now being to your Erik,' he said in his lilting accent.

Yes, I thought, *good it is that you appreciate it*, for more than ever now I was convinced that my best chance of surviving this ordeal, or at least of preserving Angelina's wretched body for whenever she eventually returned to it, was to make a friend of my jailer. And if I could not actually get him to change sides – unlikely, in that Gregory was probably paying him quite a lot of money for his services – then at least I could evoke some feeling of sympathy inside him for me which might prove helpful.

Also, if Erik began to believe I had now become a passive little pawn in this game, there was at least the hope that he might drop his guard and relax the strictness of the regime. Not that I had any real ideas with which to form a coherent strategy, for I also had not the slightest inkling of where I was save for the fact that I was being held in a recently constructed stone hut in a small compound somewhere in the woods of the Hacklebury estate. But just to get clear of my captors would be a start. The finish, if there *was* to be a finish, would have to take care of itself, if Meg did not take care of me first, that is.

And so I curled up against Erik's trunk-like thigh and cajoled and coaxed new life back into his member, if not apparently into the rest of him, which seemed content to relax and allow me to continue with my demonstration of submissiveness. Neither did his cock seem in any great hurry to return to full wakefulness. After several minutes, however, I had it all but giving me its full attention, so I leaned over his lap and took the gleaming head into my mouth. After that, it took but a few seconds more of my ministrations to get him fully erect again.

Erik, the rest of him, that is, did not seem in any great hurry to make use of the results of my labours. Instead, he closed his eyes completely and sighed heavily again, patting me on the head as if I were a spaniel that had finally grasped the idea of a trick. 'Good girl,' he murmured. 'Keeping this is what you must now be doing nice and hard and warm and wet in your sweet little mouth.'

My 'sweet little mouth' was in danger of losing its 'little' status if I was to make a habit of employing it in this fashion, for my lips were distended and distorted to accommodate his huge shaft. Yet I remained diligently at my task and worked steadily up and down his length, at least I worked up and down that first third of his penis that was all I could actually get into my mouth.

After a while, I thought I could detect a soft snoring sound. Damn the man, had he dropped off in the middle of all this, and with a hard-on from which you could have flown a fair sized flag? Was this the chance I was waiting for, presenting itself at such an early stage? However, I hardly dared risk stopping yet for fear the change in sensations might bring him back to wakefulness. Besides, there was still the matter of the leash from my collar, the other end of which remained tightly wound around his hand and trapped inside his clenched fist.

And then all thoughts of possible escape were banished, if they had ever truly been there.

'Ah, such a sweet tableau!' Meg exclaimed from where she stood in the open doorway, her hands on her hips, grinning wickedly down at me, the gleam in her eyes one of sheer malevolent triumph at what she obviously took to be the initial stages of my final humiliation. 'What a good little sucker you are, Angelina. The master should be here to see this, but unfortunately he is away on business this afternoon and won't be returning until evening.'

There was something in the way she imparted that little gem of information that made my heart sink, for violent in his ways as Hacklebury was, he was at least as predictable as any man could ever be, whereas Meg was definitely a criminal lunatic and, with her in charge, almost anything was likely to happen to me. However, I was not about to give her any more satisfaction than she had already gleaned by surprising me in my current position. I simply stared blankly up at her and continued to suck Erik's cock. Not, of course, that she would have been able to detect any facial emotion on my part, but I think I also managed to keep my feelings from my eyes after an initial second or so of surprise.

'Very good, Angelina.' She took half a step forward. I felt my spine tingle with growing apprehension, but she halted again and returned to her pose of hands on hips. 'Perhaps I shall have you in my bed this evening,' she said. 'That mouth seems hungry, and I can find it a different diet for a few hours.'

My mind flickered back to my present-day encounters with Anne-Marie. What Meg was suggesting was nothing I had not done with my new friend once she introduced me to the basics of all-girl sex, but somehow the thought of lying with my head buried between this woman's thighs, and being made to suck and lick her pussy, felt a world away from anything we had done in twentieth century Hampshire.

'Lick like the good little doggie, you are,' Meg said, 'like a hound, all brown and sleek. Perhaps we should get you a tail, and more.' She paused, pursing her lips. 'Yes, indeed, what a good idea, I shall give you to the master as his very own little lap dog. That will amuse him greatly, I think, though first we must see to it that you are properly prepared and trained.'

Oh, Lord, I thought as I continued giving Erik's staff my full attention, *what in the world has got into the bitch's malicious head now?*

I did not have to wait long to find out. But first there were other ordeals in store for me. Although Meg soon left me to my self-appointed task, my respite was not to last much longer.

Chapter Two

'Poor Teena,' Anne-Marie cooed, stroking my knee consolingly. 'It must have been terrible for you.'

Andy, still dressed in his Andrea mode, had refilled my glass and now passed it back to me.

I sipped gratefully, the burning cognac tracing a line of warming fire down my throat when I swallowed. 'It was,' I agreed, 'but in a way completely different from what I might have been expecting, a way I can't really even begin to explain.'

'Well, it wasn't your real body,' Andrea pointed out.

I shook my head, partly in agreement but partly to indicate that my transvestite friend wasn't getting the point, and neither was she likely to. 'It wasn't,' I confirmed, 'but in a way it was, at least it was the only body I had for the time being, and I had no way of knowing whether or not I would survive to come back to this one if I was still in that one when it was killed.'

'Of course you would have,' Andrea insisted. 'It stands to reason that if your body here is still alive, then so are you.'

'Shut up, you daft bitch,' Anne-Marie snapped. She took my hand in hers and squeezed it, attempting to show me that *she*, at least, was trying to understand. 'It's easy enough for you to go all scientific and clever here and now, but Teenie was back there then.'

'Yes,' I said. 'There was little enough room for anything

other than trying to figure out how to stay in one piece and try to get away from them. Besides, it's a moot point as to where exactly my life force, if that's the right term, would be. Did I carry on breathing while I was out cold?'

'Just about,' Anne-Marie replied. 'Very shallowly, though, and very slowly, like someone in a coma, I suppose. But that's not the point now, is it? Tell us what happened next. Or would you rather rest a while?' she added, as if suddenly appreciating the fact that my adventures in time might have left my nineteen seventies self in need of a recovery period. Her eyes, however, betrayed her eagerness to know more, and quickly.

'No, I'm okay,' I said, shifting my position against the pillows. 'Just give me another ciggie and I'll carry on with the story.'

As I said earlier, my actions with Erik seemed to be being carried out by a third party and I was little more than an observer. But in the meantime, the central core of my brain was active on another tack. As I stroked and sucked Erik's cock slowly back to full attention, I was trying to work out some logical line to what was happening, and why.

Gregory Hacklebury had employed a look-alike to take Angelina's part in a so-called marriage ceremony, presumably because Angelina would have been no more willing to give him the nod in front of a priest than I would myself. Therefore, as far as the world at large was concerned, Angelina was now Lady Hacklebury. Presumably, the doppelganger was still being used for any public appearances. But then again, was she?

I considered what I knew of this period. Ladies were

45

frequently 'out of sorts' for all manner of reasons, and if the public had been informed that Sir Greg's new spouse had taken to her bed with some form of ladies' ailment, the likelihood of any eyebrows being raised was remote. Which meant the situation regarding the doppelganger was irrelevant.

I set myself to concentrating on the facts, the facts, Teena, just the facts.

Okay... so the world thought Greg had a legitimate wife and that wife came with a healthy dowry. A disgustingly healthy dowry, from what I had gleaned before. Greg thus had his hands on the family money and on anything else of Angelina's he fancied, including her body, which was currently being occupied by yours truly. However, he seemed only marginally interested in her body, beyond the fact that he seemed to get off on it being physically abused and on shagging it as he so thoroughly had in his bedroom.

On the other hand, Greg already struck me as the type to whom one fanny was much the same as another, and a serious shagging was a serious shagging regardless of who was on the other end of it, if you pardon the expression. Besides, the mad maid Meg also seemed to have some hold over him and considered that cock of his as being primarily her domain and only 'on loan' to his supposedly legal wife.

And there was another 'besides'.

I had been incarcerated in this apparently specially built prison in the woods and given over to a living, breathing and almost comically well endowed version of the Swedish Chef. And unless my personal Viking was going against direct orders, part of his remit included going through my service manual on a daily basis. Given that Meg must have realised she had come upon us not long after my latest 'overhaul' and had not sounded or looked as if she was at all upset by the fact, I concluded that my personal bits could not therefore have been off limits to the giant Scandinavian and, moreover, that Meg at least, if not Hacklebury himself, was actively encouraging him to roger the living daylights out of me.

Given what I knew of Victorian birth control methods – hit and miss and then only if you were lucky seemed to be the order of the day – there was thus a very serious probability that my virile minder was going to plant a lasting memory inside me, and not just in my mind. Unless, of course, he was in some way sterile, but then I doubted they had the technology back in this here-and-now to be sure of that, so I dismissed this from my list of factors and posted it onto the one marked 'remote possibilities for later consideration'.

So… neither Hacklebury nor Meg could be worried about my eventually giving birth to a little blond bundle. Or maybe Hacklebury might be and this was just part of Meg's ploy to make sure I did not establish any position of favour with her beloved master. She was certainly possessive enough of him to consider something like that, but if I did end up conceiving courtesy of Erik and the resulting offspring turned out to be his spitting image and Hacklebury had indeed not wanted that result, he would surely turn against Meg for betraying him. Wouldn't he? What was happening to me probably had to be happening with his full knowledge and consent, the question was *why*. And then a thought struck me, a thought which, as I tried to work it through to its logical conclusion even though logic in such an illogical set of circumstances tended to run its own course, sent a chill through me.

What if Gregory Hacklebury needed Angelina pregnant? Maybe the initial marriage dowry was only part of it and there was more money and perhaps even more land coming to him on the production of an heir. It was the sort of thing that happened back in these times and still happened in the twentieth century, for that matter.

Yes, that made a lot of sense, I realised. Angelina gives birth, doctors confirm the arrival of the baby, Hacklebury cashes in his second set of chips, and then...

Then he no longer has any need of either Angelina or the child and *that* was the chilling bit about the whole concept. Infant mortality rates in Queen Vicky's day were quite awful, as were deaths in childbirth, and whilst Gregory undoubtedly would need the child to survive the birth and be pronounced healthy in order to claim the rest of his wife's dowry, would he need Angelina any longer? I shuddered to think of the fate that awaited any illegitimate infant once Greg and Meg had their hands on the last of the loot. It would either be 'disappeared' or die of some mysterious infection, poor little mite. I blinked back tears for my as yet unborn baby, but then realising what I was doing, I shook my head fiercely and tried to dismiss such sentiments from my mind. After all, this was all only just so much conjecture; the truth was probably a mile off.

Or was it?

By this time, my ministrations had aroused Erik as fully as it was possible to arouse any man. And as his shaft throbbed in my gloved fist, he now regained far more interest in its possible re-employment. Only too aware that the people around Hacklebury appeared to regard serious amounts of ropes, chains and straps as a main ingredient in the recipe for satisfactory sex, and wishing to spare myself further sessions bent double or strung up in mid-air, I decided upon a pre-emptive strike.

Without waiting to be asked, I drew myself up onto my knees and quickly straddled Erik as he lay propped against the wall, fumbling as best I could with my hampered fingers to guide him into me. After two brief and clumsily ineffective attempts, I succeeded with my third effort and sank down onto his monstrous erection with that stomach filling sensation I now knew so well.

He grinned at me and raised one finger to trace a line down my leather-covered nose. He then opened his massive hands and grasped me around my slender waist, his fingers and thumbs all but touching thanks to the strictures of the corset I still wore beneath the bodysuit. 'Erik's little dolly,' he said softly, lifting me slightly and then lowering me back over him again.

I let out a whimper and felt myself starting to go limp, for that was exactly how I always became in his grasp. Inside this diminutive body, my individuality laced away inside the featureless leather skin, I was indeed nothing more than a doll as, fully recovered now from his earlier efforts, Erik proceeded to play with me.

I was lifted and lowered over his shaft, worthy of a god in Valhalla, at a languid pace, but each deep thrust was doing its inevitable work. Very soon I felt the heat rising inside me and the debilitating tingles and spasms in my belly began anew. My head lolled back and my arms hung loose at my sides, my eyes hooded not just by the mask now but also by my half closed lids. Reality flew out the door and I gave myself over completely to the sensations swiftly overwhelming me. His penetrations felt so unbelievably good, even though I knew there was little enough emotion involved in the performance. I moaned and groaned, whimpered and simpered, and my head rolled from side to side. I was not tied down this time but I was just as helpless and thus I felt free to grant this body what it seemed to enjoy, and myself the liberty of sharing in that pleasure. I began to come and continued to come, over and over again, orgasm after orgasm flowing together as my sex gushed in response to its energetic filling, until the barren room was no longer there and images I could not even begin to describe were swimming before my eyes and inside my head... until consciousness and dream became as one and I hung in mid-air and in mid-existence and cared not whether I lived or died...

When I finally regained some sort of self-possession, I felt as if I had in fact died or wished perhaps that I could.

I must have passed out completely at some point for I came around lying in the straw flat on my back with my legs spread wide. When I tried to sit up, a jangle of metal links told me that a chain leash now ran from my collar to a ring set in the wall. Of Erik there was no sign.

Every joint in my body was aching with a fierceness I could scarcely believe – my knees, back, neck, elbows and shoulders – and inside I felt as if I was on fire, my stretched muscles sending burning messages of protest to my brain for the torture I had allowed to be inflicted upon them. I groaned, rolled over and got myself onto my hands and knees as a precursor to attempting to stand up, although why I felt the need to regain a vertical position I had no idea.

My throat was dry, my mouth still free of the gag, and I longed to get to the jug of water that stood in a corner, but I could as easily have crawled to it as walked. Perhaps something inside me was insisting I crawl for such a basic requirement and was surrendering to its animal status. But should I have cared by now? If this weird crew were out to break me, they were certainly going about it the right way and were well on the road to succeeding.

I managed to raise the jug between my hands and gulped gratefully at the contents, which tasted surprisingly fresh and cool. And yes, I did walk across the little room even though it required a tremendous effort to regain my feet. It was even more of an effort to effect the few short steps required, for I still wore those silly high-heeled boots and my balance was as badly off form as my joints and muscles felt.

After what must have been at least two pints of water, consumed I hasten to add in three or four separate gulping sessions, I realised I badly needed to pee, not from this recent intake but from an earlier one and as a result of everything else that had happened since. The cool air told me I was still unlaced over my private parts. With little or no other options open to me, I squatted in an ungainly fashion, my back against the wall for support, and let the river flow, closing my eyes in a futile effort to block out the sound of urine splashing into the straw between my feet.

'Very good, bitch.'

I groaned inwardly for it was Meg who had spoken, her timing immaculate to catch me in such a degrading position. I opened my eyes and there she was in the doorway, her hands as usual on her hips, her features contorted by a grin that was all sheer malicious triumph. With my mouth empty for once I was tempted to make some retort, but apart from the fact that I could think of nothing suitable I was quick to realise that any show of spirit or resistance on my part could lead only to even worse retribution than anything she undoubtedly already had planned for me.

'I… I had to go,' I stammered, trying to get back to my feet even as the last dribbles pattered down into the straw.

Meg's grin widened. 'Of course you did,' she agreed 'and like all bitches, you went on the spot. That's very good, bitch, and you'll learn a few more things before I'm through with you. I've had a word with the master and he likes my idea. Even now his man is preparing your new skin for you. It should be ready this very evening and I shall take the greatest delight in displaying you in it. Meanwhile, I have given Erik some strict instructions for the rest of your day and he will be back as soon as he has eaten and bathed. The great oaf smells of you, you whore,' she hissed, but I could see the fact pleased rather than angered her. 'Bitch in heat, that's all you are now, sweet little Angelina.' She paused and stroked the side of her jaw for a moment, considering. 'And that name simply won't do,' she concluded. 'Such a ladylike name for a doggie girl just simply won't do, so we shall have to find a more suitable one for you.' She snorted something between a laugh and a cough and spun on her heels. 'I shall spend the afternoon considering it,' she called back as she swept out into the open air. 'Yes, we must find a proper name for a proper bitch.'

In the right era and in the right circumstances, mad Meg could have earned herself a fortune. She seemed to have a perfect grasp of what was needed in order to humiliate and control people, and there are always plenty of men and women who are prepared to pay fortunes to suffer such treatment in such imaginative clutches. I, however, do not count myself among their numbers, but then I wasn't being given any choice in the matter. Nor was I given any choice by Erik when he eventually returned.

He carried with him two slats of wood and for a moment I thought he might be intending to use them to paddle my backside, but no, for he also had with him two lengths of some sort of canvas strapping. These two pieces of timber were, as I quickly discovered, intended for a far more devious purpose.

Grasping my right arm first, he extended it horizontally and lifted the first piece of wood up against my forearm, winding the strap about it with his other hand until he had established it enough to employ both hands to continue winding the binding down as far as my wrist and up, until my gloved hand was also held immovably against the splint with some twelve to fourteen inches of the wood still projecting beyond it.

My left arm and hand were quickly treated in identical fashion whilst I stood like a statue trying to work out what he was doing and what the planks were for. Of course, when the answer came it was obvious for all the clues had been there previously, but it still came as a horrible shock when he ordered me down onto all fours, legs straight, the tips of the splints acting now as extensions to make my arms approximately the same length.

'Doggie girl,' he said, chuckling, and indeed I now must

53

have resembled a greyhound in many ways although I moved, when instructed, with considerably less grace, of that I am sure. For several minutes, Erik made me walk back and forth so I could coordinate my legs and arms, until he was apparently satisfied with the result. 'Walk now outside we shall,' he announced, and produced a leash he snapped onto my collar before he stooped down and peered into my face, hot and red with shame behind the mask. '*Woof* you will say,' he instructed.

I swallowed and blinked, but there was nothing much else for it. 'Woof,' I repeated dutifully.

He patted my head. 'Good doggie,' he said, looking pleased. 'Later a bone you shall be getting if good girl you are.' He shook the leash and gave it a short tug. 'And now walking we shall be, for sunny it is and fresh the air, too.'

Outside, as I made my clumsy and undignified way, I could see no sign of Meg, but I was almost certain she had to be somewhere close by watching me with glee. Part of me wanted to stand upright again and shout out that they could do whatever they wanted to me without ever succeeding in turning me into an animal, but the sensible part told me to hold back, to bide my time and wait. For if they continued to think they were breaking my spirit, then perhaps they would relax their vigilance and present me with a chance to escape, though how, when and where was another question altogether.

Our progress through the trees was slow and I wanted to shout that we could go a damned sight faster if only he would let me stand upright, but I knew the answer that would bring. Meg had decreed that I was to be treated like a dog and dogs walk on four legs, not two. I sighed mentally wondering just how far that woman was capable of going, but I already knew the answer. Hers was the sort of mentality that was able to justify mass murder, genocide, and the extreme tortures employed by gangsters and corrupt governments all over the world and all throughout the ages. Every terrorist regime, whatever its size, depends upon dumb followers and semi-passive supporters, but there have to be those capable of leading them, and in events like the French Revolution, the Megs of this world would not be sitting at home knitting while the heads rolled; they would be the ones working the guillotines.

It wasn't long before the two pints of water I had drunk began to make their presence felt and I knew I would have to stop to relieve myself. Tentatively, I tried to draw Erik's attention. 'Master?' I made an effort to sound suitably humble and compliant.

He turned back and pointed a finger down at me. 'Woof!' he said, almost barking himself. 'Dog say woof.'

'Woof,' I muttered.

He smiled in a watery sort of way, as if his mind wasn't really on this new game at all.

'Woof, woof,' I repeated. He chuckled and nodded, but I could see he had no idea what I was trying to communicate, and why should he? I gave up trying and instead simply shuffled my legs further apart and let it flow, trying to ignore the fact that the ground being hard and, there being no layer of absorbent straw beneath me, my leather-covered limbs would be splashed.

'Aha!' he exclaimed. 'Peeing is what the doggie girl wanted. Better feeling will you be now, I think.'

Better feeling I was, at least in as much as the emptying

of a protesting bladder is a universal feeling of relief we all need no description of, but having to pee in front of a man was not something likely to enhance my spiritual well-being.

We walked on again and all the time I was having trouble keeping my mind off one particular prospect. Peeing like a dog was one thing and certainly bad enough, but when it came to needing to empty my bowels, could I face having to squat down and do that in public as well, for that was surely the only option I would be allowed.

After a while, we came to a high wooden paling fence set atop a brick wall which I presumed marked the boundary of the Hacklebury grounds at this point. It stood more than ten feet high and my heart sank as I gazed up at it. Even with the use of my hands and with no other sort of bondage restrictions I would have found such an obstacle nearly impossible to breach, for although Teena in the seventies would have little enough trouble reaching up and grasping the timber section to pull herself up, Angelina would struggle and her fingers, even without gloves and strapped to stiff timbers, had not been designed with fence scaling activities in mind.

We turned right and followed a cleared pathway along the boundary wall for a good ways. I estimated we must have covered nearly a mile and still there was no sign of a break in the wall or even a gateway. It looked as if the perimeter was well protected around most, if not all, of its length, yet there had to be at least one entrance somewhere.

At last, after what was beginning to feel like half a lifetime, Erik halted and turned to jab a finger at me. 'Sit!' he ordered.

For a moment I was at a loss what to do, but then I realised what was expected of me. I sank down and back onto my haunches, my arms extended in front of me, the picture of obedience, not to mention stupidity. I looked up at him and saw the pleasure on his face. At any moment I expected him to produce a biscuit and have me beg for it. But no, he had a better doggie treat in mind.

Slowly, he unlaced the front of his breeches and took out his flaccid but still impressive organ, stepping towards me and planting his feet between my wooden paws. 'Good girl,' he said, pointing it towards my lips, and yes, like a good girl I parted them and accepted the offering, flicking away at it with my tongue so that it quickly began to rise and thicken. 'Good girl,' he repeated several times as I closed my eyes to try to shut out the reality of what I was doing.

But then what else could I have done? Erik carried a short crop at his belt and I knew he would not hesitate to use it if he thought I was trying to be rebellious. And even without the whip, those big hands across my bottom would have been painful enough. Besides, there was also Meg waiting back there for me somewhere, her devious mind no doubt full of all manner of spiteful tortures to inflict upon her rival, as I now knew she saw me.

It certainly took less time to bring Erik to full preparedness than on the previous occasion in my little straw-filled cell, but this time I was not permitted the luxury of taking the initiative. Instead, he tugged on my lead and ordered me up, not onto my two legs but back up onto the four. I groaned slightly, yet there was an uncontrollable tremor running along my spine and through each of my limbs as I realised he was going to take me from behind, doggie style. I just prayed he would use the right orifice and not get carried away, for his girth would be more than I could hope to deal with in my back passage.

Fortunately, my Viking knew what he liked and wanted and was not one to try new paths, at least for the moment. Grasping my hips, he allowed his shaft freedom to find its own way unguided, and that it did as he stooped to place it beneath my lower belly and then drew it slowly back until its engorged tip found my already wet little slot. *Damn this body*, I thought as he began to enter me. The brain was thinking one thing but the fanny was thinking something else entirely.

But then again, was the brain really thinking so differently? I had to ask myself that for despite the ignominy of my position was not the feel of a thick cock probing into me, and me not in any position to resist, proving to be something of a turn-on? I pushed that thought aside before it should make me disgusted with myself and gave myself over instead to the inevitable surrender of my flesh, yet again, to my giant master. And he did not disappoint me.

'He fucked you like a dog?' Anne-Marie exclaimed, her eyes wide, though not entirely, I suspected, from horror. She shook her head in a dramatic gesture that was supposed to signify revulsion but which failed to do so. 'Oh, how awful!'

'Actually, it was pretty good,' I confessed. 'After all, we've all done it that way even if it's been on our hands and knees, and once I was able to forget that I'd been made to walk there all the way in that position, well, it was as good as the time before that. And doing it that way adds *so* much extra penetration! I felt as if he was going to come up my throat!'

'Yuk, Teenie, you're disgusting!' Anne-Marie cried, but then she began to laugh and Andrea joined in.

'Well, if you don't laugh, you cry, or so my dad likes to keep telling me,' I retorted. 'I must have looked quite a sight, I suppose, but I was soon past caring about how I looked.'

'You reckon Meg was watching?' Andrea asked.

I shrugged. 'Maybe. I wouldn't have been surprised if she had suddenly come out of the woods, but then she probably had other things to do. Greg had this guy who made all manner of things, from leather corsets to that awful bodysuit, and it was him Meg was getting to sort out my new outfit to her specifications.'

'A dog suit?' Andrea asked almost eagerly.

'Don't get ahead,' I said, 'all in good time. I could do with a cup of tea first, if nobody minds.'

'There's still plenty of brandy left.' She nodded towards the bottle.

I shook my head. 'There may be, but unless you want me crashing out before I've finished, I'll give it a miss for now. I feel exhausted and we've had several already.'

'True,' my friend agreed, turning to Andrea. 'Go put the kettle on, sweetie,' she said, 'and bring in that big box of chocolate biscuits I've been saving since Christmas. I brought them with me in my pink-and-white carrier bag but I think it's still in the car.'

Actually, even if mad Meg *had* suddenly stepped out from between the trees, I doubt I could have cared less for I was resolved I would bear whatever indignities she cooked up for me and allow her to think she could beat my spirit down without recourse to any real physical punishment. Besides, all the while Erik was giving me a good old servicing trying to focus my brain on anything else was well beyond my capabilities.

Little exploding lights again… and then big exploding lights… I should probably have fallen despite the supposed advantage of having four legs for balancing instead of just two had he not kept such a tight hold on me throughout. And then I was pushing backwards to meet his thrusts with as much vigour as he was displaying, if not as much strength. I could hear the wet slushy sounds we were making, seemingly amplified through the *son-et-lumiere* that had invaded my head, but far from making me feel ashamed the sound excited me even more and I heard a weird howling sound I knew could only be coming from my own throat.

I heard Erik, too, though what he was saying I had no idea for most of it was in his native tongue and only the odd 'bitch' and 'dog' made any sense to me at all. Again, I should have been mortified to be called such names, but I wasn't, not at that moment, at any rate. He could call me whatever he wanted to all the time he was doing what he was doing to me, and as you and I both know, all the time in Erik's case was quite a long time…

I was allowed to lie on the grass for a while when he had finally finished with me while he sat nearby, leaning against a tree and regarding me with what I realised was fondness. I crawled nearer to him and would have repeated my ministrations of earlier in the day, except that now my arm ended in a piece of wood and not even a mitten of leather.

He understood and patted my head. 'Sleeping now a short time should you be,' he murmured. 'Wanting you walked the afternoon altogether she was, but good girl you are for Erik, so resting you shall be, but for long not, for searching for us she will otherwise be.'

'Woof,' I mumbled, and laying my head on his thigh, closed my eyes. I drifted into a shallow sleep, a sleep filled with dream images of me and Erik, Meg and Greg and Anne-Marie and Andrea, all of us romping through woods and all of us naked with our unnaturally white flesh covered in big black spots. All of us, that is, except Meg, who wore a full-length coat with a high fur collar and smoked a cigarette through a long holder as she sneered at us through darkly made-up eyes.

All too soon it was time to be on the move again. This time Erik made me walk ahead of him and I shivered at the thought of the picture he was now getting, my bare arse and my still wet quim jutting out behind me framed by the dark leather. When he reached forward and patted my damp pussy, I knew he was not entirely unappreciative of the spectacle.

By now I was beginning to get some idea of the size of the Hacklebury estate. Even allowing for my slow progress in the all-fours mode, we had been walking, following the perimeter fence, for maybe four or five miles in all, and the curve of the boundary was so slight that I calculated it would take us several more hours at the very least before we had covered even one quadrant. History was my strong subject, much more so than maths, but even I was able to work out that, unless there were some sharper corners in the fence, the woods within the wall had to cover a good few square miles.

As I plodded on, I was thinking.

If Gregory Hacklebury had owned such a large-sized plot of England as recently as the eighteen thirties, he and his family must have been pretty powerful, or at least well known, and yet I had been unable to unearth any record of the bastard in my research. How, or why, should that be? Had something happened that prompted local historians to expunge all trace of him from their histories?

It seemed unlikely, not so far forward in time, relatively speaking. By the nineteenth century, records were being kept in something approaching a modern form and often with a zeal that would otherwise only be found in train spotters, and it would have required more than just a local conspiracy to bury all traces of a man and a family who must have ranked pretty high in the league of landowners.

I felt another pat on my bottom, but it barely interrupted my latest train of thought. I considered other possibilities, some of them promising, others falling more under the category of idle speculation.

Perhaps Hacklebury himself did not actually own the land. Perhaps he was some sort of minor relative, a nephew or a second cousin, something like that, and the real owner was away helping to conquer the growing empire. Maybe he was nothing more than an employee, a steward keeping the place going for a travelling master. Maybe Hacklebury wasn't his real name at all... but no, that would never do, and besides, most of these possibilities made his determination to marry Angelina somewhat strange and improbable. An heiress would not be permitted to marry a mere steward, and neither was it so likely that her guardian would permit a wedding with a minor relative.

And besides, I knew he was a Sir, or at least all the staff I had met so far seemed to believe he was.

It was all very curious, I thought as the hard-baked ground with its smattering of browning grass continued to pass beneath me. Could he have won this estate in some game of chance? That may have sounded ludicrous at first, but I knew that sort of thing went on between young men in this century. The modern day equivalent of millions of pounds changed hands on the turn of a single card. If Hacklebury had won the estate by gambling, and then perhaps was to lose it again within the next few years, perhaps that might explain why his name did not appear in connection with any large acreage by the time I was searching for information on him in the nineteen seventies. It would take time for deeds of ownership to be registered with the appropriate authorities and, whilst these early Victorians were noted bookkeepers, things moved very slowly by comparison with my own era.

A jerk of the lead to one side indicated we were to turn off the perimeter pathway now and head straight down another path we had come to that headed back, I presumed, in the general direction of my little compound. A mile or so on, we reached an area where the trees thinned to either side for a hundred yards or so and the cleared ground was covered with a far thicker carpet of grass that was actually green rather than the fading colour it was elsewhere.

Erik tugged backwards on my leash and issued a single command for me to halt. My continued display of swaying feminine bits must have had its inevitable effect on him; without further ceremony or warning, he grasped me by the hips and entered me again. Immediately I felt myself responding to his thrusts from deep within the uncontrollable centre of my flesh, which had been my nemesis from the first moment I was transported back in time into this body. But even as the tide began to rise, I could not help wondering if this was now to be my lot for whatever was left of my life here – to be treated as something less than human and to be used at the whim of whoever happened to be on the other end of the chain clipped to my collar.

This time, my body's strength was found wanting and despite Erik's solid support my knees soon buckled. Sensing I could no longer hold myself up, he allowed me to sink slowly to my knees, following me down without ever slipping out of my cloying pussy. Then, as I knelt with my head touching the ground, he continued to pump in and out of me until I was once again moaning and writhing in the throes of an overpowering climax.

To my surprise, Erik's latest assault did not last anywhere near as long as the earlier ones. After what could have been no more than five minutes at most, he withdrew from me without coming himself. He allowed me a few moments to recover something resembling composure, and then lifted me back into my earlier proscribed position.

'Every hour or so, say she,' he informed me with yet another pat of my bottom followed by a sly stroke across my slippery nether lips. 'Wet she says to be kept you must and wet are you for sure.' He chuckled. 'Wet think I you always are anyways,' he added, 'but hurt it does not sure to be.'

I knew that if I ever had the chance I could easily throttle Meg even given the diminished strength of this body of

Angelina's, for real hatred can generate miraculous feats and now I knew I truly did hate that mad woman. I felt utterly helpless and totally abased by the simple way in which she could order me to be screwed at regular intervals simply to make sure I stayed wet and presumably ready for whatever it was she was planning for my next ordeal. To be shagged without having any say in the matter was one thing, but to be so merely as a form of self-lubrication...

Images of black-clad maids swinging from nooses with their tongues lolling from bloated purple lips swam before my eyes. It was an automatic response that made me move forward again at Erik's command, for my thoughts were no longer on the path we were following. Meg would pay for this one day, of that I was now determined. Whatever she tried to inflict upon Angelina, I would keep the poor girl's body alive until we were both avenged. Justice, I swore, would come to both Meg and the man behind her madness, even if it were to be a justice never recorded for posterity, as neither of them had apparently passed into the annals of history. I grimaced as I considered a picture of Erik ramming into Meg as she lay across a rock with her legs clad in black stockings kicking in the air, her cruel lips gaping open around cries of agonised protest...

No, I told myself firmly as I let the tableau fade, that punishment was far too good for her. When the time came I would find both the strength and ingenuity of purpose to repay mine, and Angelina's, debts to her in a full and appropriate fashion.

By the time we finally came back within sight of my little prison complex, I realised the afternoon was growing quite late for the shadows from the trees were stretching across the little clearing and the sun was low enough that I could no longer see it above the trees. I calculated that our walk must have occupied a total of six or seven hours, if Erik's timekeeping accuracy was to be relied upon; he had stopped to have his way with me no less than three more times and it had been the better part of another hour since the last session.

By now my earlier mood of grim determination had by and large given way to a mood that was approaching a black depression brought on partly by sheer fatigue and by the aching in my back and shoulders, and partly by the growing realisation that whatever contest might transpire between Meg and myself, I was playing under the severe handicap that was the warm and seemingly ever hungry little slot between my legs. It was like being fitted with a button that anyone could press to instantly deprive me of my normal logical senses. And the more times it was pressed, the more radical were the changes it wrought in me.

I knew I should not dismiss the thought that Meg had already become aware of this fact. Despite her supposedly low station in life, the woman was as cunning as she was inhuman and probably a whole lot cleverer than her supposed betters, to boot. Hacklebury might consider himself master, but it was Meg who was truly mistress here, even if only she and I were as yet aware of this.

I expected Erik to continue his regular cycle as soon as we were once again under the roof of my prison, but instead he simply hitched my leash to a wall ring and moved outside to open the door of another small cell which I had not yet seen the inside of. I heard a rattling of metal and a sloshing of water followed by the scraping sound of something being dragged across the ground. Then he returned and, to my surprise, began unlacing the back of my bodysuit and peeling the damp leather off me. My corset was next, followed by my gloves, and then, for the first time in what seemed like days, I stood naked. Despite the fact that my giant keeper had seen just about everything there was to see, my hands went protectively to my crotch.

Erik smiled and reached out to grasp me by the top of my left arm. 'Come,' he said. 'Smell it is you do and bathing time is now.'

For one foolish moment I conjured up thoughts of a nice warm bath all soapy suds and sweet- smelling oils. It was a ridiculous hope that was dashed the moment I was thrust forward into the last stall. Smaller than the other two, the centre of the space was dominated by a small platform of wooden slats nailed across two cross-timbers with narrow gaps between them. From the ceiling above them dangled two lengths of chain, each terminating in a broad leather manacle into which Erik quickly buckled my wrists so that I was forced to stand with my arms held high and wide.

As he secured me, my eyes fell upon the row of four metal buckets that lined one wall and were each filled almost to the brim with what was obviously water. Then, without further ceremony, the first bucket was used to douse me completely, drenching me from head to toe in an icy shower that had me dancing on the spot wailing and shivering in protest.

I was washed down thoroughly with a rag cloth and something that might well have passed for soap in a stable; it smelled terrible and made my eyes water. Then Erik produced a cutthroat razor, which he used to hack off my hair and shave the stubble until my skull was as smooth as my bottom. I stood helpless while he did this, a combination of shock and the realisation that nothing I could say would stop this latest desecration, keeping me dumb throughout, but I did give a little yelp when he began to lather the blonde triangle between my thighs.

'Still you must be keeping,' he admonished me firmly.

My eyes flickered fearfully towards the gleaming blade in his hand.

'Cutting you will I not be if moving about you are not.' He sounded confident but it was a confidence I did not share. However, I managed to close my eyes and hold myself rigid while he worked away at removing my sparse and fair pubic growth.

'Done we now are,' he announced shortly.

I let out a long breath I had been holding, and staring glumly down I was just able to see the very top of my pussy lips now that they had been deprived of their little curtain. I had not seen a sight like that between my legs for a good few years now and I felt a tear well up as I thought of the warm safety of the bathroom and bedroom back home at my parents' house.

'Miss Meg coming soon will be,' Erik said, picking up the second bucket of water. This time, he poured it over me with a little more care but the chill was no less and I found I was now shivering continuously. I tried to divorce my mind from my body again, concentrating on Meg and how I might yet be able to outwit her. It would not be easy, even if it were at all possible.

She had called me Buttercup when I was first laced into the bodysuit, telling me that I was now no better than a calf or a deer and worthy of even less consideration, but earlier today she had apparently forgotten that and referred to me as Angelina, albeit only to say that such a name was unsuitable for a bitch and that she would have to come up with a replacement. I already had a rough idea of what she was planning as the next stage in my humiliating enslavement, but I suspected she would probably be a little more inventive than Rover.

At last Erik released my wrists and led me back through into the main cell, where he allowed me to sink down onto the straw to rest my aching muscles and joints.

The respite was not to last long, however.

Within minutes, Meg arrived as expected accompanied by Polly, the maid I had encountered before, and a third maid I had not met yet and whose name, it transpired, was Betty. Both younger girls carried small sacks before them, which they placed carefully on the floor just inside the doorway. The newcomer was nothing special but she was sturdily enough built and had about her that same dullish air Polly displayed; like Polly, she would follow orders and like Polly she would do only what she was told. Unlike Meg, who did the telling and gave the orders, she would never consider thinking for herself.

'My, but don't she look funny with all her hair gone!' the new girl exclaimed. 'Like a ghost she is!'

I felt my cheeks burning at this and lowered my eyes even as Erik reached down to haul me to my feet.

'Hush your mouth, you stupid girl,' Meg admonished her, 'otherwise I'll have Erik do the same to you.

Understand?'

'Yes, ma'am,' the young maid mumbled, and I heard Polly just fail to stifle a snort of laughter.

'And *you* can be quiet,' Meg snapped, her hearing no less keen than my own. 'Pottinger delivered enough things today for you to end up playing the cow for a while, and see how that suits you!'

'Sorry,' Polly said meekly. 'Didn't mean nothing, I'm sure.'

'Right, well, cut your cackling and get her into the suit, and make sure you lace everything good and tight.'

'What about her corset, ma'am?' Polly asked. 'She had a corset before, so shouldn't she have one this time?'

'No need now,' Meg retorted. 'Pottinger has added stays in the right places and he assures me this is as good and tight as any corset could be, maybe even tighter.'

I felt my stomach turn over at this announcement, for although I had become accustomed to that corset, this short spell of total naked freedom had reminded me just how terrible a garment it really was, and now I was about to be subjected to something that was regarded as even worse.

It was Polly who produced the new suit from her sack. At first sight it did not look to be any different from the one into which I had been laced before. However, as it was brought over to me, I could see there were one or two innovations that had been added and the most noticeable, I discovered as my feet and legs were forced down into the leather tubes, was in the feet. For a start, the boot part had been adapted so my feet were arched even more cruelly than before, while on the outside some clever stitching and artful padding contrived to give the impression of two huge paws. I winced as much with shame as discomfort as the two maids pushed and pulled at me, tightening laces that ran up the outside of each of my legs until the dark-brown leather was stretched to the contours of my limbs and buttocks like a second skin. I could feel without looking that once again my bottom hole and sex were left uncovered, the tight leather compressing my nether lips into a pout that made them even more prominent than before.

'See to her hands first,' Meg instructed.

The maids then each produced what I took to be boxing gloves at first, but as they curled my hands into tight fists and forced the leather over them, I saw that the padding extended only to cover my fingers from the first knuckle joints to just beyond the second. Laces were drawn tight and knotted and now my hands were even more useless than they had been before, two shapeless little balls at the ends of my arms. I stared down at them and made no protest when the women began pushing them into the sleeves of the suit.

Almost immediately I recognised the practicality of these mitts. The sleeves of the suit, I now saw, were much longer than my own arms and ended in paws identical to those on which I now stood, the extra length being made up of some solid filling within the last twelve or so inches of the tubing, atop which sat some form of hardened leather cup against which my curled fists were to rest. The padding was designed to give at least some relief from the constant weight my fists would be bearing, a concession that probably owed more to the practicality of Meg's intentions than to any sympathy for my discomfort.

The suit was hauled up over my shoulders and the lacing at the back began. I felt my already slender waist being compressed even more cruelly, forcing the air from my lungs and evincing involuntary gasps of pain from me. Staring down at myself, I saw that I now appeared to have a much more prominent bust than before and concluded that the carefully stitched breast cups had been substantially padded to produce this effect.

I felt myself growing giddy from lack of oxygen, but Meg had anticipated this and stepped forward to thrust a bottle of something acrid smelling beneath my nostrils. I gasped and blinked away the tears that sprang into my eyes, but the woman was unsympathetic.

'You should know how to breathe properly by now,' she snapped. 'Get a grip on yourself or I'll take a birch to your arse.'

I fought against the automatic feeling of panic and eventually succeeded in re-establishing a pattern of short, shallow breaths that soon enough helped me back to normal sensibility. By now the lacing had continued up to a point just below my neck, where Meg ordered a halt. I felt one of the girls tying off a knot and then Polly stepped away and crossed over to her sack.

'No, not that, not yet,' Meg barked, seeing something dark and bulky emerging. 'Get her new tail first. I want her mouth free for this, and I want to see her face.'

This announcement filled me with dread for I guessed immediately that if the sadistic bitch wanted to see my reactions, then the tail was not going to be something I was going to appreciate.

Someone, this character Pottinger, presumably, had gone to some lengths in the quest for reality. The tail was maybe two feet long in total and apparently made from a tube of stitched leather into which padding had been forced to give it a proper three-dimensional appearance. However, there must also have been something else hidden inside, presumably metal or whalebone, for it curled in a manner that would have been quite pretty had it been the tail of a real dog. I saw that the thicker end was mounted onto a circle of thicker leather and that from this extended two straps, the one very short and the other much longer, which then divided into two quite separate straps in the form of a letter V. But what really drew my attention was the gleaming leather phallus that sat around the longer strap where it was still single and could clearly be adjusted, attached as it was by means of a leather loop that ran along the strap.

'The short end goes onto the buckle above her arse,' Meg instructed as Polly moved around behind me.

I closed my eyes as I felt her fingers fumbling to make the attachment, and so I was unprepared for someone grabbing me by the nose and jerking my head downwards.

'Bend over bitch,' Meg hissed, 'and stay like that. I'm going to do the rest of this myself.'

And do it she did. Thankfully, the dildo on the strap was neither long nor thick for it was not intended for my sex but for my other orifice. Even so, although Meg paused for a moment to add a lubricant to it, it was a painful entry and remained painful for a minute or so, until my muscles grew accustomed to its presence and relaxed around it.

Meg, however, was not waiting for such niceties. Instead, she passed the strap through my legs and drew the left side of the V up to a small buckle that awaited it on the front of my bodysuit. The second half of the harness was likewise buckled and, as it was tightened, I realised it had been specifically measured and tailored so that, although my backside was now plugged and obscured, my pussy remained completely unobstructed and available for any and all.

'There!' Meg exclaimed, stepping around before me once more. 'Yes, that really is splendid. That little man really is an artist. Don't you think so, Erik?'

Erik, who had been quietly observing events from what was the nearest thing here to a neutral corner, grunted and nodded his head but his expression betrayed nothing of what he was really thinking. Was he merely thinking of later, when I would once again be completely under his control for my hourly fucking? Or did he perhaps feel a little sympathy for me as he watched what these terrible people were doing to me?

'Turn around, dog girl,' Meg commanded.

Slowly, still far from steady on my new footwear, I obeyed. I could feel the weight of my new tail behind me and a slight tugging as it bobbed with my movement, a tugging that was amplified several times when it reached the shaft that was now held tightly within me. I let out a little whimper and gritted my teeth against that other sensation which this movement immediately began to awaken in my traitorous flesh. *Damned stupid body!* I thought fiercely. Even a fake cock up the arse had it starting up all over again!

'Very pretty,' Meg said approvingly. 'But get onto all fours, like you've been trained to.'

To be honest, it was something of a relief to lean forward and take some of my weight and a lot of my balance onto my newly extended arms. I stared down at the paws, fascinated by their shape and by how real they appeared. At the same time, and for the first time, I realised I could no longer bend my arms at the elbows. A combination of the tight lacing of the sleeves and stiffened leather about the joints had deprived me of even the slightest flexibility. As I experimented, as discreetly as possible, I realised the same was now also true of my legs. From now on and until I was released from this insidious invention my progress would be very stiff-gaited, something I was sure Meg had contrived to add to the comic humiliation of my overall appearance.

'It's almost funnier to leave you like this,' she murmured, running a hand over my smooth pate. 'However, Pottinger has come up with a true masterpiece for you and it would be a terrible shame to waste it. Polly, see to her mouth first, and be quick about it.'

Now, over a period of many years spread across many centuries, I have endured gags of all shapes, sizes and construction, from simple wads of cloth to sprung pears of polished wood that threaten to dislocate the jaw, but the method that was now employed to deprive me of articulate speech was among the most cunning and has been passed down through the decades, as I will relate to you in another story. Quite simply, this gag was a short, flat piece of polished metal, which was pressed across my tongue and attached to two small clamps that settled over my back teeth. Then, by means of tiny little screws tightened by what we would nowadays call an Allen wrench, the clamps were tightened so there was no chance of me dislodging them with pressure from my tongue. The overall effect left me with the power to make all the sounds I wanted, except that none of them would now sound human. Furthermore, the metal gag also left my mouth available for other things, always supposing that the person availing himself of it did not mind the abrasion of metal on their quite tender flesh.

Now satisfied that I could no longer protest my humanity, Meg produced the *pièce de résistance* of which she had spoken. Although my eyes widened with horror as she held it up for me to see, I could not but admire the ingenuity and craftsmanship that had gone into its creation. Basically the same as the hood mask I had been wearing before, it differed in two areas only, but those differences made all the difference, as it were. The front of the mask had apertures for the eyes, but from that point downwards it had been shaped into the form of a pug-like snout complete with a black nose and an opening beneath it that led to my mouth, although the integral stuffing meant that the dog mouth was an inch or two ahead of my own. On either side of the hood had been sewn two large and floppy brown ears I could see would loll with every movement of my head. Furthermore, without the handicap of my hair, the whole mask could now be laced tightly to my features, so that it would sit snugly and immovably about my head, a head that would now not look out of place on any canine bitch.

The hood was quickly fitted to me, the back lacing extending down the collar beyond the nape of my neck, and then the remaining lacing of the bodysuit was continued so it covered even that. Finally, a bright red leather collar, beset with gleaming metal studs, was locked about my neck to both protect the lace knots from interference and to ensure that my neck remained stiff

76

and straight.

'Marvellous!' Meg exclaimed, clapping her hands with delight. 'I only wish we had brought a mirror so you might see yourself, but never mind, for there are mirrors enough in the house and I intend that you shall indeed see what a wonderful prize I have created for the master's pleasure!'

Chapter Three

'She turned you into a fucking dog?' Anne-Marie looked horrified, but again I could see the undercurrent of excitement in her eyes.

I put down my cup and regarded my new friend and lover sombrely wondering if she was secretly wishing it had been her, my usually so dominant lesbian, in that awful animal disguise. My Anne-Marie... was she a closet submissive who could not bring herself to admit to it? Idly, I resolved to test that possibility at a more appropriate time. 'Indeed, she did,' I replied, reaching for another cigarette. 'And she added ankle cuffs and chains up to the front of my collar to make sure I couldn't stand upright if I was ever left alone.'

'And what about your new name?' Andrea chimed in. 'Did she remember about that? Did she come up with one?'

'Oh, yes,' I said, smiling awkwardly. 'She remembered, all right.'

'Sheba,' Meg declared, 'although I must admit that at first I considered it rather too regal a name for a bitch slut like you. But then I remembered a bitch that the head gamekeeper here once had who was brown and skinny and very obedient. So, *Sheba*, will you bark for your mistress, or shall I have Erik thrash you like the bad dog you really are?'

78

'Woof,' I said sullenly, but that half-hearted attempt was nowhere near good enough for Meg.

'Bark properly,' she snapped, slapping me lightly along one side of my snout.

'Woof! Woof!'

'Louder!'

'Woof!' I bellowed.

'Again!' she shouted.

Again I did my dog impression.

Meg's head rocked back and forth with laughter as the two maids joined in her merriment. I saw Erik stirring slightly and a moment later realised he was anticipating Meg's next order. 'Right, fuck the bitch, Erik,' she said. 'And you, my little bitch girl, you'll bark your head off while he does it. I want to hear you bark and whine, otherwise I'll find a real hound to put you to, and don't think I wouldn't!'

I didn't think she wouldn't, not for one moment, and so as Eric once more slid into my unresisting tunnel, I bucked my doggie hips and rolled my doggie head and whined and snuffled and barked for all I was worth. And in the end, I must confess, I had lost all control of myself and any claim to human dignity whatsoever.

All the while Meg looked on with eyes that shone with triumphant malice knowing she had already succeeded far beyond her wildest dreams in breaking me, and that her position with Hacklebury was becoming more secure and less threatened by my presence with every passing minute and every added ignominy to which I was now incapable of doing anything, it seemed, than submitting to like a bitch in season.

It was to be another two or three hours before I was finally paraded before my supposed husband. He was dining with guests, Meg informed me with a smirk of satisfaction, but I would be the star of the after dinner sojourn, and no doubt about it. For my part, I believed I had now gone beyond caring about anything other than my eventual revenge upon this witch of a woman. I as yet had no further ideas as to how I was to escape her clutches, but I remained firm in the belief that my chance would eventually come. After all, I reflected grimly, every dog is supposed to have its day.

Hacklebury sat with five other people as Meg finally led me into the long drawing room. One of the guests was a female older even than Meg, quite possibly in her fifties, although a thick layer of make-up made it difficult to gauge her age accurately. The other four guests were men all attired in the tight breeches and cut-away formal jackets visible in a thousand pictures of the age. They were all smoking small cigars and, judging from the redness of their cheeks, were all well on the way to being drunk. A near empty decanter of what I guessed was brandy sat on a low table in their midst as further evidence of their over indulgence.

'So, what have we here?' Hacklebury asked loudly as I straight-legged my way through the door at the end of my leash. The four men all turned to squint in my direction as the woman lifted an eyeglass on a silver stalk.

'My word!' she exclaimed, and I could see from her change of expression that she was genuinely surprised. 'My word, but what a creature!'

'This is Sheba, sirs, ma'am,' Meg announced, leashing me to a halt and dropping into a half curtsey. 'She's the thieving little wench we caught trying to climb in through the pantry window,' she lied. Obviously, my true identity was not for this public's consumption. 'She was offered either the courts or service,' Meg continued, probably making the story up as she went. 'Of course, they'd have hanged her if she'd gone the other way, this being not the first time she's been caught trying to steal from the house.'

'Indeed, they would have,' the oldest looking of the four men agreed. 'Always thought that was a bit of a waste myself, but then maybe you've started something here, eh, Hacklebury? Tell me, do you reckon she'll make anything of a guard dog? I doubt she'd move fast enough for the hunt.'

'Indeed not, my lord,' Hacklebury replied, smiling, 'but she moves fast enough for our purposes here, I'll warrant. Guard dog I don't know, but house dog most certainly.' He stepped forward and carefully walked all around me, stopping to flick at my proudly curled tail and to stroke the sleek hide of my flanks. He came around again to stand before me and then squatted down to peer into my face, particularly fascinated, it seemed, by the mouth in my mask. 'Quite remarkable,' he muttered, extending two fingers to probe the opening. If the artificial mouth had possessed teeth and been under my control, I think I should have snapped the intrusive digits off, but of course it did not and neither did I have any such control over the inanimate extension to my face. 'This is very good work, Pottinger,' he said.

Behind him, I saw a portly little fellow step forward, his face wreathed in satisfied smiles. 'As I told you, Sir Gregory,' the man who I assumed to be the architect of my latest shame said smoothly, 'my usual clientele require nothing less than perfection and this is not the first such mask I have made. In the East they even have their creatures hunt and draw carts and they are kept for years in stables and kennels just like the real thing.'

'Well, this creature has her kennel all right,' Hacklebury said, standing upright again, 'and by all accounts she is becoming very quickly accustomed to it, eh, Meg?'

'Indeed, she is, sir,' Meg confirmed. 'Unfortunately, however, the bitch seems to be permanently in season.'

'Ah, very interesting,' said another of the men. He was quite thin, with hawkish features and nothing to particularly commend or distinguish him though his accent suggested he was from the upper classes and had probably never done a day's decent work in his life. 'The bitch requires a dog? Or do you already have one for her, Hacklebury?'

'A Great Dane, you might say,' Hacklebury answered, and laughed at his own wit. 'A veritable giant of a dog quite capable of satisfying a dozen such bitches, but if you feel the urge to give it a go yourself, Mellam, then by all means, be my guest.'

The woman, who had been listening to these exchanges with an amused expression flickering across her features, now stepped forward. 'What say you, Mellam?' she demanded, prodding at his shoulder with a long finger. 'Fancy giving us all a show, do you?'

Mellam seemed somewhat flustered by this latest turn of events, but the woman did not appear to be about to let him off the hook on which he had unwittingly impaled himself.

'I mean, just look at the poor little bitch,' she said. 'Why, she seems to be panting for it. Doesn't she, Gregory?'

'She seems to be panting for something, I agree.'

Hacklebury turned and grinned at Mellam. 'But I think our friend here is just a little put off by your presence, Margaret, or maybe he thinks his weapon may not be up to the job. Here, Mellam,' he continued, grasping the thin man by the arm, 'come around here and see what awaits you.' He led his guest behind me and I knew without looking that he was pointing down at my exposed and shaved quim, the lips of which were being forced into a tight *moué* by the V-strap. 'Look, they're blowing you a kiss of welcome, Mellam.'

Margaret and the other men all chuckled at this and promenaded around me so they could see this degrading sight with their own eyes.

'If I were a man and possessed of the necessary,' Margaret said evenly, 'I don't think there is any way I could ignore such an obvious invitation. Go on, Mellam, give the bitch a little of what she wants, there's a decent chap, and don't mind me. Why, I'll even help you get your pole up, if it needs help.'

Mellam was not at all keen, that much was easy to tell, but the others were now set upon having him take me. Although the chiding and protests went on for several more minutes, perseverance aided by further quantities of brandy soon had Mellam stripped below the waist. Margaret was indeed as good as her word in rendering assistance and stepped forward to grasp his drooping tool, but her ministrations weren't really that necessary for within seconds, now that the die was cast, Mellam proceeded to grow an erection that would have done almost any man proud – almost any man who wasn't Erik, that is.

For my own part, I knew I was already wet and I could

feel the now familiar heat spreading out from my sex long before Mellam was ready for me. He himself sounded quite surprised when he placed the head of his weapon against me. 'Damn it, but she's certainly hot and ready enough!' he exclaimed, as much in a show of bravado as anything else, I guessed. I felt him push forward and, despite the compressive factor of the V-straps, he entered me easily enough, sliding his full length into my proffered pussy with a single thrust.

'How is she, Mellam?' Margaret enquired. 'Is she good and tight?'

It has to be a tribute to the elasticity of vaginal muscles the world over that Mellam announced to the little gathering that I was indeed tight enough for his satisfaction despite my recent experiences at Erik's hands, or rather at that other part of his anatomy.

'Take her nice and slow, Mellam,' Hacklebury advised. 'Make it last while we all have ourselves another drink.'

I heard Mellam grunt as he thrust in and out of me and I was glad once again of the anonymity afforded my own facial reactions by the mask. I was not surprised when I found my body yet again reacting of its own volition, my hips pushing backwards to meet his penetrations as little gurgling noises emanating from deep within my throat emerged from my gaping dog's mouth.

'She's an obliging bitch, I must say,' Mellam declared breathlessly. His hands grasped my hips to steady himself and I realised he was no Erik; he would probably discharge into me quite soon despite Hacklebury's warning for him to take it steadily. As I panted and groaned in rhythm with his hips, I supposed that the sight I presented would have been too much for the self-control of most men, so it was no surprise at all when I felt him erupt inside me with a choking cry.

'You need a drink, sir,' Hacklebury said, strolling back across the room with a glass held before him.

Without withdrawing from me, Mellam apparently accepted it because I heard him gulp the fiery liquid down hurriedly. Only then, with his shaft already beginning to wither inside me, did he have the courtesy to remove it, leaving me with a feeling of emptiness and, much as I hate to admit to it, disappointment. But as I ground my top teeth down onto the clamps that held the gag strap across my tongue, I doubted I would be left unsatisfied for very long...

'Eventually, after they had all had their fun with me, Pottinger included, Meg took me back outside, handed me over to Erik, and he took me back to my stall,' I concluded my story. 'I thought maybe he was going to have one last dip at me for the night, but it must have been the early hours by then and I reckon he was pretty whacked out himself. He gave me a drink of water poured down a metal funnel, of all things, and then told me to lie down, threw a blanket over me and left me to sleep. I dropped off pretty much straightaway, and then... well, then I woke up back here.'

'What an ordeal!' Anne-Marie exclaimed. 'It must have been horrible to be treated like that.'

'It was,' I admitted, 'and yet something was happening inside me that made it all seem quite surreal, and even...' I hesitated. 'Well, it was almost enjoyable, though in a quite impersonal way,' I added hurriedly. 'After all, it wasn't really my body and that funny crew mostly didn't

85

even know who I was supposed to be, let alone who I really am.'

'I think I know what you mean,' Anne-Marie said slowly. 'That's part of the whole bondage and submission thing. Once you're tied up and you've given over all control to someone else, you can just go with the flow. Of course,' she said by way of qualification, 'in normal circumstances, that control is surrendered willingly, whereas you weren't given any choice in the matter. And what am I thinking of?' she exclaimed suddenly. 'There you are still sitting there in that tight corset. It must be killing you by now.'

I peered down at myself. I was still dressed in the elaborate Victoriana garb I had donned for our earlier games. I shrugged. 'To be honest,' I admitted, 'it doesn't really feel that tight any more, not after being laced into that damned dog suit thing. That really *was* tight, believe me.'

'I think we should get you out of it, all the same,' Anne-Marie insisted, 'and then I reckon we'd all be better off at my place. Your cottage is really quaint but there's no denying the plumbing here leaves a lot to be desired and the sleeping space is limited. Besides, so far you've been here when you've been whisked off on your travels, and while we don't know for sure that's a factor, the fewer chances we take, the better, at least for the moment.'

'I agree,' I said. 'I'm not saying I don't want to go back and sort that bitch Meg out, but not just yet. I feel as knackered now as if it was this body that was going through all that and my head's starting to throb. Plus, there's a few other things I need to get straightened out.'

'Like finding out a bit more about Gregory Hacklebury,

for instance?'

'Yes, that for one, but then there's been these other things... I didn't mention them before, but I have these sort of half remembered images floating around up here.' I tapped my temple. 'Some of it is Angelina stuff, but there's other things as well, and I need to try to focus on them.'

'Well, tomorrow you can focus all you want,' Anne-Marie said, rising. 'But for now, we'll get you into something more comfortable and I'll drive us all back. Then in the morning, dear Andrea here can do us the biggest fry up in history and sod our waistlines.'

I slept alone for what remained of the night and well into the following morning, waking only when the smell of bacon frying penetrated the jumble of my dreams through the half open bedroom door. I sat up, shook my head to clear it and swung my legs over the side of the bed knowing I needed the toilet before anything else. I stopped only to snatch up a terry cloth robe that was hanging over the back of the bedside chair.

Downstairs, still heavy-eyed and clad only in the borrowed robe, I found Anne-Marie about to pour coffee and Andrea, neat and precise in a white mini dress and opaque white stockings, turning bacon and sausages in one giant pan while several eggs sizzled in another hardly less impressive skillet.

'Hungry?' Anne-Marie asked, tipping hot liquid into the first of three mugs.

I nodded, pulled out a chair from beneath the kitchen table and eased myself down onto it. 'Starving,' I confessed, my mouth watering. 'I feel like I could eat a horse.'

'Well, we've got the best part of half a pig over here,' Andrea said cheerfully, 'but no horses, I'm afraid, so you'll have to make do. Baked beans and mushrooms okay for you?'

It really was a dietician's horror of a breakfast, complete with buttered toast, fried bread and even fried tomatoes, the whole laid out on plates that were huge in comparison with anything we'd ever had at home. But within minutes the feast had been devoured, leaving only greasy traces and not a guilty expression in sight.

'That's the way to start a day,' Anne-Marie sighed, and reached to replenish the coffee mugs. 'So,' she continued as we added our individual sugar and milk quotas, 'what's on the agenda for today?'

'I'm really not sure,' I confessed. The fry-up and coffee had brought me fully awake but I had no more idea of where I should try to go next than I'd had the previous evening. 'Like I said, we've found no Hacklebury references to do with large estates, so there has to be a reason for that, and perhaps that's where we should try to start.'

'Except we don't have the name of the estate, nor even where it was,' Andrea pointed out. 'Don't you have any idea at all, Teenie?'

I shook my head. 'I had the feeling that it had to be in the south of England, quite possibly in either Hampshire or one of the adjoining counties, but I never saw anything much that would offer a real clue and it could just as easily have been somewhere up north. It was fairly warm, but then it was summer and even Yorkshire has warm days in summer. It's not all Bleak House and snow drifts, you know.'

'Well, given that my family Hacklebury connections are all in Dorset,' Anne-Marie said, 'then I reckon it would be reasonable to assume that your first guess is fairly close to the truth. Whether it was a Hacklebury who owned this place or not, we should start with the estate itself and work backwards from there. It's a shame you didn't think to try to get something more out of that lot while you were back there. Even a village name might have been a start.'

'I did have other things on my mind,' I pointed out just a little too tersely, 'and half the time I wasn't able to speak, even if I'd thought of it.'

'No, of course not,' she replied quickly. 'But it might be worth trying to keep that in mind for next time… always supposing there *is* a next time, of course.'

'Oh, there will be,' I said, and somehow I knew, with an unshakeable conviction I could not explain, that my time-travelling adventures had only just begun.

Chapter Four

Quite what I hoped to gain from identifying the true position I had fallen into at the Hacklebury estate I was not quite sure, except that I had always been brought up to believe knowledge means power and the next time I came face-to-face with Gregory and his mad henchwoman I would need every scrap of power I could muster.

Besides, I reasoned as we drove along the coast road towards Dorchester, if I could identify the estate I might also be able to discover why it was that Hacklebury's name was no longer to be found anywhere in association with any large area of property. In this fact I felt sure lay at least part of the key to all this. The longer I thought about it, the more positive I grew that the land had probably never been rightfully his in the first place and that he had usurped the title to it as surely as he had usurped poor little Angelina's dowry along with everything else that should rightfully have been hers.

Gregory Hacklebury, I was now convinced, was a form of Victorian land pirate, totally unscrupulous and completely without any human principle or compassion, but still weak enough to be manipulated by a female psychopath whose hunger for wealth and position was probably fiercer even than his own. Meg was the true mistress of the estate, as I should have seen from the beginning, her maid routine and public obsequiousness no more than a sham, and even Gregory knew that, I now suspected, though for some reason or other he found himself unable to break free of her spell.

'It's almost like she was a witch,' I muttered as we crossed the county border into Dorset and began climbing a hill from which the view out over the English Channel was as spectacular as it was peaceful under the surprising winter sun. 'She was definitely the boss in that set-up.'

'Yes, only presumably Hacklebury assumed she was his faithful hound in much the same way as she tried to turn you into her obedient little dog girl,' Anne-Marie sounded distracted; she was squinting against the glare from the chalky deposits that covered the asphalt road here.

'Yet every dog must have its day,' I murmured, repeating the thought I'd had some one-hundred-and-thirty years back in time. 'Only a sensible dog doesn't bite the hand that feeds it, not until...' I slapped the dashboard with such violence that Anne-Marie swerved sharply towards the centre of the road. It was lucky there were no vehicles approaching in the opposite direction or my enthusiasm might have ended our quest right there and then.

'What the—?' she gasped.

'That's it!' I cried. 'Um, sorry,' I muttered as an afterthought. 'But that's the answer, the reason why Greg's name isn't down on any title deeds we've been able to find. The land was never truly his and he never succeeded in getting it, not legally or any other way.'

'You mean—?' Andrea began from the backseat.

'Meg! Yes! *She* got it all in the end.'

'And what happened to Hacklebury?' Anne-Marie asked, half turning her head towards me while concentrating on the road.

I shrugged. 'Who the hell knows?'

'Or cares?' Andrea added.

'It might explain a lot, certainly,' Anne-Marie conceded. 'But unless I'm mistaken, we don't happen to know anything much about this Meg, aside from the fact that she was a psycho.'

'And a hell of a lot cleverer than Hacklebury, who seems to have done most of his thinking with his penis,' I said. 'Like most men, as it happens.' There was a slight cough from behind us. 'Present company excepted,' I added, turning to look at the demure female figure sitting with her long legs elegantly crossed and her dark Cleopatra-style wig as immaculate as a coiffure could ever hope to be. 'Besides,' I added, grinning, 'I thought you were in girl mode today?'

'I am,' Andrea pouted, 'but a girl has to defend her roots.'

'Huh,' Anne-Marie snorted, 'I always *dye* mine.'

'Let's get back to Meg,' I suggested. When I get an idea I like to pursue it hard and fast and this was a good strong line to follow.

'She never mentioned a surname, I suppose?' Anne-Marie prompted.

I shook my head. 'If she did, and I'm pretty certain she didn't, then it went straight past me.'

'Then we're not that much further on, are we?' Andrea observed.

Anne-Marie was far more positive. 'I think we could be,' she said encouragingly. 'Before we were chasing Hackleburys and now we're coming down here to chase suitable sized estates, only right up until a few moments ago we had nothing to help us decide which estate might be the right estate, given that we already know there were no large properties registered to a Hacklebury of any description.'

'So, we just go over all the old maps and records for Dorset, Wiltshire, Devon, and the whole of the south of England while we're at it?' Andrea made no attempt to hide the sarcasm in her voice.

I held up a hand. 'No, wait a bit,' I said, screwing my face up in an effort to concentrate. 'Let me think a moment... maybe we can narrow it down after all.'

'Take your time, sweetie.' Anne-Marie stepped on the gas to overtake a crawling Morris Minor estate.

I looked sideways and pulled a face at the three young children who were pressed against the rear window and making their own variety of faces at us as we sped past. 'Meg definitely wasn't upper class and neither did she sound particularly middle class,' I began, 'but then she could have come from anywhere and it doesn't follow that she had to have been born wherever it was we were. Hacklebury could have picked her up anywhere on his travels, or vice-versa. But those other maids had to be locally born, and their accents were pretty rural, although not strong enough to be real west country. Get as far down as Devon and Somerset and the accent is really thick in the country, and I reckon it would have been thicker still back then without radio and the telly to take the edges off.'

'So, Hampshire or Dorset, you think?' Anne-Marie prompted me again.

'Yes, and not that far north in either county,' I concluded. 'Go up thirty miles and they speak as broadly as anyone

93

from cider country.'

'Along the coast, then?'

'Maybe, but maybe again, not quite.' I nodded left towards the sea, which was perhaps half a mile away now as the road moved slightly inland. 'Open the window and take a deep breath,' I suggested.

'Smells of petrol and bird shit,' Andrea said in a most unladylike tone of voice.

'Smells of salt,' I corrected her, 'what people wrongly refer to as ozone. We all know that smell and yet, because we live near the sea, we take it for granted. Our family home is only a few hundred yards from the shore, so the smell is particularly strong there, but when the wind is in the right direction you can catch a whiff of it inland for a few miles, even at the cottage in Rowland's Castle.'

'What about seagulls?' Anne-Marie prompted again. 'We often hear them when they come inland. Did you hear any screeching up above when you were back in time?'

'No,' I replied after a moment, 'but then seagulls tend to drift inland mainly when the weather is a bit dodgy, or they sense a storm brewing, and all the time I was back there it was as flat and calm as it is today and a whole lot warmer. It was midsummer and the sea would have been like a mill pond.'

'But even so, if you'd been within a mile or two of the coast, you'd have heard something,' Anne-Marie persisted.

I conceded that she had a point, especially as it fitted in with my own recently formed and still evolving theory. 'So,' I went on, 'I reckon we need to concentrate on a corridor of land stretching east to west over... let's say fifty or sixty miles, and from a point about five miles inland to somewhere around thirty miles north of that.'

'Oh, that'll make it easy then,' Andrea piped up again.

I turned and glared at her. 'I'll do something to you that means you'll stay a bloody girl forever if you don't shut up!' I snapped. 'Just pay attention, will you? It's not going to be quite as much needle and haystack as you seem to think. After all, we're looking at an area of maybe eighteen-hundred square miles, which sounds a lot but isn't, not really, not when you consider that most of the country in the area would have been open farmland and what I saw was largely woodland, and lots of it.'

'A large wooded estate in the middle of the farm belt then,' Anne-Marie declared, nodding. 'Yes, you could be right, Teenie, and if your theory about the accents is on the money, this might take a lot less effort than we thought.'

I make no pretensions to genius, even if my intelligence level is comfortably above average, but I've always prided myself on being able to think analytically and even laterally. I'm also pretty good with cryptic crosswords and even better at them when I'm drunk, but that's beside the point here. I've also always had this ear for voices, which made me quite a good mimic during my school days, and now this dubious talent, which earned me a few detentions in my time from unimpressed teachers, finally paid off.

In the main library at Dorchester, pouring over a large map copy dated eighteen forty-five, we found three promising possibilities within minutes and a further check through musty records volumes delivered the final goods.

'*Megan Crowthorne*,' Anne-Marie read out loud. '*Registered title of Great Marlins Estate in eighteen forty-*

one from the previous owner, one Saul Carpenter. Doesn't say how much she paid, if she paid anything at all.'

'Any other details about her or this Saul Carpenter?'

'Not here,' Anne-Marie said, shaking her head. 'This is just the bare on who owned what. We'll have to delve into parish records if we want more.'

'Why not try going back further and finding out who Saul Carpenter got the place from or if it was in his family for years before that?' Andrea suggested, becoming sensible and positive for perhaps the first time since cooking our breakfast.

'What if Hacklebury was really Saul Carpenter?' Anne-Marie mused. 'Maybe he changed his name?'

'If he did, then it was after the time I was last there, I'm sure. No, I reckon Carpenter was a different guy and we need to find out more about him.'

It took another hour but then we had him, and with his family records came the answer to at least another part of the conundrum.

'*Saul Jacob Carpenter, born eighth of May, seventeen seventy-five, married Daisy Hacklebury at Melingford Parish Church, tenth July, eighteen-hundred,*' I intoned, reading from our accumulated notes. '*Two children, Rachel and Ruth.*'

'Good Jewish names,' Andrea remarked, chuckling, but she shut up when we both glared at her.

'No sons though, so our Gregory wasn't directly related,' Anne-Marie stated.

'He'd have been Gregory Carpenter if he was,' I pointed out.

She nodded. 'So he came from another branch of the family, maybe a brother or a nephew of Daisy's.'

96

'And he was after the estate once Saul died, is my best guess,' I went on. 'What year did it say he died?'

'Eighteen thirty-seven,' Anne-Marie answered, consulting her notebook. 'And we know Rachel Carpenter predeceased him by six years in that typhoid outbreak, but we still don't have any record of the dates of death of her sister or mother.'

'Which presupposes they must have moved away before they died,' I concluded.

'Leaving behind three thousand-plus acres of prime country estate,' Andrea muttered. 'Not so likely, I think.'

'Unless you consider what two women, one of them by that time quite elderly by the standards of the day, would do with three thousand acres of woodland and a couple of hundred more of tenant farms,' I said. 'I reckon cousin Gregory came on the scene about then and made them an offer they couldn't refuse.'

'Using the money he knew he would get once he married Angelina,' Anne-Marie added. 'But what about his title? You said they all called him "sir", didn't you?'

'Yes, and what idiots we are!' I exclaimed. 'That's the one place we haven't checked and it's so obvious I can't believe we missed it. There's a list of titles, isn't there?'

'I thought we checked that at Portsmouth library?'

'Yes, but that list was only of hereditary titles, those that have been passed down from father to son. There have always been things like life peerages and lifetime only knighthoods, especially the ones that were bought from whatever government was seeking to raise money at the time. A few grand could have you dubbed a sir in weeks, from what I've read.'

'Well maybe,' Andrea said, 'but we ain't gonna find no

such list in this sort of dead and alive place. We need somewhere like Somerset House for that.'

'Or the British Museum,' I suggested.

'Somerset House, British Museum, it's all the same to me,' Andrea said. 'They're both in London.'

'So,' I said, sitting back and stretching my cramped shoulders, 'who's for a day in London tomorrow? Carnaby Street isn't what it used to be, but there's always King's Road if we find what we want soon enough.'

'Some chance of that,' Andrea sniffed. 'We'll be all morning on the train and all afternoon stuck in some dusty reading room. The shops will all be well shut before we get a crack at them.'

'Then we'll book a hotel and stay a few days,' I said. 'It'll be my treat and a reward for all the help and friendship the pair of you have shown me since we met.'

'And there's a certain little club I think you might like, Teenie,' Anne-Marie added, grinning. 'You know the place I mean, don't you, Andrea, dear?'

London in the mid nineteen seventies wasn't quite London in the early or mid nineteen sixties, but then I'd been little more than a tot during the heyday of Carnaby Street and the first invasion of the miniskirt, so I wasn't able to make any accurate comparisons and the London into which we arrived was still a swinging enough place in its own way.

My money pit wasn't exactly bottomless but it was deep enough and I had originally intended to treat my two friends to a few days in the best luxury money could buy, but then Andrea insisted on travelling as Andrea rather than Andy and Andrea's taste in hemlines and footwear was likely to get us thrown out of most of the higher priced hotels for attempted solicitation of the guests, so we settled for a lesser, although still very comfortable, establishment on the boundary of Fulham and Chelsea just a short tube ride from the centre of the city and close to the fashionable nightspots of the day.

We travelled up on the train to Waterloo – even in those days the thought of driving in the capital was more than any of us could bear – and took a taxi to the hotel, where we spent a couple of hours settling in and snacking on the bar menu. By then it was already past two o'clock in the afternoon but we resolved to at least make a start on the reason for us being there. Another taxi ride later, we were in Somerset House, home of the records of every hatch, match and dispatch that had ever been recorded anywhere in Britain.

Now, I think that at this point, and especially for younger readers, I ought to explain that nineteen seventy-five, even though only a little over a quarter of a century ago, was still very much pre-computer age, at least as far as the great majority of the country was concerned, and what might nowadays have taken the three of us no more than an hour, had we spread our efforts over three individual terminals, was likely to entail a day's hard study and even then we were not guaranteed results. Everything back then was large ledgers, scruffy index cards and that marvel of modern data storage, the *microfiche*. Cross-referencing and trail following had to be done manually and fuzzy matching happened only at the end of a long day when the brain was just about at the end of its tether. That having been said, we did quite well in those few hours left to us on our first day in London.

Gregory Hacklebury, appointed as a Knight of the Order of St Basil by the then Prime Minister, Lord Melbourne, in November of eighteen thirty-five. Of course, the records didn't say just how much that cost dear Gregory, but it probably paid for at least one new warship, we were all agreed. What this particular record did not reveal was when our errant knight died, but that could wait until later.

Following the trail backward, we discovered that Gregory Hacklebury was the son of Simon Hacklebury, brother of Daisy, who had become Mrs Carpenter and lady of the estate Gregory had obviously set his cap at. We also discovered that Ruth Carpenter had married one Lieutenant John Hample, whose date of demise was given as eighteen-fifteen, the day of the Battle of Waterloo. There had been, or so it seemed, no offspring from the union.

'So,' Anne-Marie concluded, sitting back and doodling idly in the margin of the pad upon which she had been tabulating our findings, 'by the time we move on about another twenty years there are just the two Carpenter females and no children to inherit. Meanwhile, Daisy's nephew has somehow contrived to get himself a title and presumably makes an offer for the estate, possibly offering a down payment with a promise of the balance to come once his title and lands have worked the oracle to enable him to marry Angelina and grab her dowry.'

'That would make sense,' I agreed. 'Daisy would want the family estate to stay in the family, I suppose, and as long as she and Ruth had enough to live out their days in comfort, she would be happy enough with the arrangement. But I wonder where mad Meg came in? I had assumed Meg was a short form for Margaret, but

Megan is Welsh, isn't it?'

'Doesn't necessarily follow,' Andrea said. 'Andrew was the patron saint of Scotland but the nearest I've been to haggis bashing land is probably Nottingham.'

'It was a bit different back then,' I remarked. 'Names tended to reflect areas and local fashions and Megan is definitely a Welsh name.'

'Maybe Gregory went Taffy side for a bit and wound up with the manic maid on his travels,' Andrea suggested.

'I'm not sure that where he found her is important, at least not for our purposes,' Anne-Marie said. 'What we do know is that she ended up with the land and, presumably, whatever was left of Angelina's money.'

'But we don't yet know what she did with Great Marlins since it doesn't appear on any modern day maps other than as a little hamlet called Marlin Cross,' I pointed out. 'She must have sold it off in sections and it was all split up, although maybe the house is still there under a different name.'

'I still can't see why we're doing all this,' Andrea protested. 'We know Gregory didn't get what he wanted, so why bother?'

'Because, we still haven't found out what happened to Angelina and why Meg ended up with the booty,' Anne-Marie replied before I could do no more than open my mouth. 'This is Teenie's family, we think, and she seems to think she's going to end up going back there again, so it's quite possible that if things went tits-up for Gregory, Teenie, as Angelina, might well have played a key part in that, so she needs to know everything we can find out.'

'It's getting late,' I said, glancing up at the clock, 'and it's been a long day. Why don't we leave it for now and start afresh tomorrow? I could do with a hot bath, a nice meal and maybe a couple of bottles of wine.'

'Sounds good to me.' Anne-Marie scooped up her pens and pencils and dropped them into her purse. 'And then there's a little nightspot I'd like to show you, the place I mentioned yesterday, which I'm just certain you're going to love!'

Chapter Five

Bon D'Age. Okay, it wasn't subtle and it certainly wasn't any wordplay in any language I could confirm from my own admittedly limited knowledge, but then it didn't have to be either and the sign was above the inner door and not out on the street, where the main entrance was a plain, black-glossed door set back in an alcove between a second-hand shop and a very old-fashioned looking gentleman's outfitter.

Just inside the inner entrance, we were stopped by two bouncers in suits who might have given Erik a run for his money, but Anne-Marie produced a small card and we were quickly waved through and down a corridor lit dimly by red lamps, the black painted walls and ceiling reflecting very little of their illumination. We seemed to walk forever, but eventually we came to another door, which opened upon our approach to admit us into a wide foyer where there was a counter and an archway with a sign above it indicating it was the cloakroom. Tall, overly made-up but otherwise stunningly attractive girls manned both the counter and the cloakroom and another hulking brute hovered in the vicinity of another doorway that obviously led into the action.

The scene beyond that door was, well, not quite as bizarre as it might have been, for although a fair proportion of the people inside the club were clearly intent on displaying as much of their unorthodox personalities in their outfits and choice of fabrics as possible, there was a decent percentage of patrons who were dressed in a manner that could be considered relatively normal. For my part, I was almost conventionally attired in a silvery mini-dress, black stockings and not-too-extravagant high-heeled platform shoes. Anne-Marie's red suede skirt and plunging top, combined with red suede knee-high boots, would also not have turned more than the usual male head. Only Andrea – as over the top as ever in a leather miniskirt and matching halter, with stocking tops showing at her hemline and spiky heels in silver with glittering mock jewels all over the buckles – was at all outlandish given the usual dress code for a night out in the seventies.

A statuesque brunette, her all but black hair clearly owing as much to the bottle as to nature, dressed in an ankle-length, figure-hugging dress of what I quickly realised was black rubber, glided over to us on heels that made even Andrea's spikes look modest. Blue eyelids and black liner combined with glitter to produce a localised lightshow every time she blinked and her dark purple lipstick was at once scary and sexy. 'Annie!' she exclaimed, leaning over to hug Anne-Marie. 'It's been weeks, darling!' She straightened up and regarded Andrea and me. 'Hmm,' she purred. 'Well, little miss cocky drawers I know, of course, but who's this darling girl?'

Anne-Marie introduced us. The Amazon was called Carmen. I suspected her real name was probably something more along the lines of Helen or Sally, but she certainly looked more like a Carmen and I could see immediately that she had taken a shine to me, if only because I seemed to be the only female in the place who came anywhere near to matching her in height.

'Nice legs,' Carmen whispered close to my ear as she guided us towards the bar, 'but those heels are a bit clumpy. Leave the heavy platforms to the lads, that's what I say.'

The smell of her rubber dress, combined with her own musk and whatever heavy scent she was wearing, assailed my nostrils and drove deep into my senses, so that I felt half drunk even before she passed me the exotic-looking cocktail. Don't ask me why, and please don't start blaming me for things beyond my control, but as I began to sip at the straw I suspected I was going to end up having some sort of sexual experience with this Carmen and that it would happen before the night was out and I regained the sanctuary of my hotel room.

'Are you okay with this?' It was Anne-Marie asking, close by my elbow.

I smiled at her and nodded.

'Carmen has the hots for you,' she informed me. 'I knew she would.'

'But—'

She raised a finger to my lips to silence me. 'But nothing,' she said. 'If she wants you and you fancy her, then go with it and fuck whatever anyone thinks. This isn't that sort of place, anyway. *Do* you fancy her?'

'She's very attractive,' I replied hesitantly.

'She's fucking gorgeous and we both know it. Andrea would crawl on her hands and knees to the ends of the earth for her and so might I, under the right circumstances.'

'Have you—?'

'Been with her? Oh yes, but don't worry about it. You must know that people like me have a different slant on things like that. I go where and when I like, and so does Carmen and so does just about everyone else who comes here. Otherwise they wouldn't come here, would they?'

'No,' I admitted, 'they probably wouldn't.'

'Look, if you'd rather go, if all this is a bit much for you, then say so. I shan't mind, although Andrea will probably stay here till the death.'

'No,' I said, 'I'll stay.' After all, what could this place offer that could frighten someone who had been helpless in the hands of mad Meg and her motley crew?

I was about to find out.

Unlike a lot of clubs, both back in the seventies and nowadays in the new millennium, the volume of the music was kept at a level that enabled people to talk to each other without recourse to shouting. When we took our drinks off into an empty alcove we were able to talk quite normally while we watched the steadily thickening crowd.

As I said earlier, more than half the clientele were dressed much as we ourselves were, definitely not for walking the shops but nothing outlandish by clubbing standards of the day. However, interspersed amongst this show of normality were a growing number of blatant fetish outfits – rubber, leather, the shiny vinyl we call PVC nowadays, high boots with high heels, long gloves, masks, feathered headdresses, metal jewellery and chains.

'How do they have the front to travel here like that?' I asked, agog at the spectacle.

Beside me, Anne-Marie laughed. 'Some of them are out-and-out exhibitionists,' she said, 'but not all of them arrive dressed for action. There are changing areas and even a wardrobe here of things for people who can't afford to buy their own stuff outright, or who worry about keeping that sort of thing at home. We can go through and see if there's anything that takes your fancy, if you like?'

'I… I'm not sure,' I replied. 'Maybe later.'

'Well, if we want to go into *Sanctum* then we can't go unless we're appropriately dressed.'

She had said *Sanctum* in a way that made my eyes narrow. 'What's *Sanctum?*' I asked.

She smiled. 'It's the real club area,' she explained. 'This is just a sort of reception room, though some people are happy enough to stay here and just watch and dance a bit later on. The proper action takes place down below and you either have to be a member in good standing or have a suitable sponsor to go down there. Plus, you have to be dressed properly, as I just said.'

'I take it that means rubber or leather?'

Anne-Marie tapped the side of her nose. 'Or nothing at all,' she said, 'apart from the necessary chains or what-have-you, of course.'

'Of course,' I echoed and felt myself shiver slightly, especially as at that moment a tall girl in a tight-fitting leather cat suit and towering heels strode by with a chain looped around her wrist. This chain led back to a collar about the neck of a shorter girl who wore nothing but a silvery bikini bottom and matching long gloves over which wrist manacles were locked and connected together by means of a short chain link behind her back, so that she was forced to parade her naked breasts as she walked through the throng.

As the minutes ticked by and we moved on to a second round of drinks brought by a waitress in the briefest of French maid outfits, I saw that the percentage of costumes in the club that left the wearer nearly naked was overtaking the more normal dress code. Either the later arrivals were the more adventurous or, as I suspected, people were beginning to slip away to take advantage of the wardrobe and changing facilities. I knew at that moment that we would be joining them soon, especially when Carmen appeared and beckoned Andrea to follow her. Andrea, with a flickering smile back over her shoulder, trotted off obediently in the tall brunette's imposing wake.

'She seemed keen enough,' I observed.

'I told you,' Anne-Marie replied breezily, 'Andrea will do anything for Carmen, even to going back to being Andy, if necessary. Carmen knows she can make the silly bitch do anything she wants. It'll be interesting to see what she has in mind for her tonight.'

'Carmen knew we were coming?'

'I phoned ahead from the hotel earlier and said we might be,' she admitted.

'And what did you tell her about me?'

'Only that... only that you are a very special friend and share certain interests. I didn't mention anything about... you know, the other thing.'

'Good.' I didn't really want anyone else knowing about my inter-century exploits just yet. Anne-Marie and Andrea had accepted my story readily enough, but I wasn't sure how many other people would believe me. Besides, there was enough going on around here without further complications.

'I think it's best if I'm your mistress for tonight,' Anne-Marie announced suddenly as the third round of drinks arrived.

I turned to her, my eyebrows rising.

'If we're going down into *Sanctum*, I mean,' she added. 'It'll be easier for you for your first time, otherwise you'll have to pick up on any spare subs, or else some other dom will hit on you.'

'Don't I get any say in that sort of thing, then?'

'Well, yes, but there's all sorts of complicated rules and rituals and it takes a bit of getting used to. You wouldn't want to trip up on your first visit, would you?'

'Well, no, but—'

'We don't have to go down there, not if you don't want to.'

There was a long pause as I hesitated, but I knew what I was going to decide as surely as if the decision had been cast in stone for me a century earlier. 'No, I'd like to see,' I said at last. 'But don't rush things, please. Let's finish these drinks first.'

'No hurry, sweetie,' Anne-Marie said, laying a reassuring hand on my arm. 'We'll finish these and order another round. There's plenty of time yet.'

We sat for a while longer watching and listening and in its own way this was even more surreal than being back in eighteen thirty-nine with Meg and her crew, for I guessed that most of these strangely garbed creatures were almost certainly quite normal people who by day worked as accountants, engineers, builders, secretaries, shop assistants, etc. I suspected I was probably among the youngest present but that was no more than a guess for exotic make-up and masks obscured more than just identities, so that I began to feel increasingly exposed sitting there in my disco party dress wearing nothing more than a bit of eye-shadow and lipstick.

'I'm ready,' I said abruptly and gulped down my nearly

109

full glass in one very unsophisticated swallow. I stood up, tugged my hem down into place and took a deep breath. 'Now or never, I think!'

Anne-Marie nodded, appreciating that I was hovering on the brink of indecision. She took my hand as she rose and squeezed it reassuringly. 'Come on sweetie,' she whispered. 'Let's go give you a whole new identity.'

The door to the rest of the club area was set back in its own curtained alcove. Although it appeared to be unguarded, a masked face looked out at us from a glass-fronted kiosk window. Whether the face was male or female I could not tell for nothing was said and no attempt was made to stop us.

We walked down a short corridor beneath more red lamps and between the same black walls before turning left into a much longer and wider passage lined on both sides by doors set at intervals of perhaps eight or ten feet.

A girl with white-blonde hair that fell in a straight cascade over her shoulders, which were enticingly bare above a tight red corset and a matching mini skirt, walked towards us. 'Number twenty-two is empty,' she informed us, smiling with carmine lips to reveal one gold tooth amidst a row of perfectly white ones. 'Do you need any help with wardrobe?'

Anne-Marie assured her we did not and we moved on until we arrived at number twenty-two. The small room was rectangular, with a bench running along one side and hooks set into the opposite wall from which hung black plastic sacks with drawstring necks. Some of these were clearly full but the majority hung flat and empty.

'Get stripped off and put your things in one of these,' Anne-Marie instructed me, indicating the sacks. 'Don't

110

worry about security. Nobody here would dream of stealing anything. The consequences would be awful for them and they'd never be allowed back in the club, which would be the worst punishment of all.'

'And what about you?' I asked uncertainly. 'Aren't you—?'

'Of course I am,' she replied, 'but first I need to get us some suitable things. Don't worry, the wardrobe room is just a few doors down and I think I know what we need. I'll only be a few minutes.'

In fact, she was gone less than five minutes but it was the longest few minutes of my life. As I stripped, and I wasn't wearing much that required a lot of time to complete the process, I kept looking up at the door certain it would open to reveal some complete stranger. Yet at the same time I was wondering why I was worrying about that and what I was doing there if I was so worried. My mind, as you can imagine, was in something of a turmoil but then that's a situation I've since come to regard as being perfectly normal, insofar as anything in this, or any other world, could ever be described as normal.

I placed my things inside one of the empty sacks and closed the neck with the drawstring noticing that there was a small golden tag on it into which had been engraved the letter *H*. I checked the next empty sack and saw that the tag read *J* and the one after that *K*. I presumed there were similarly lettered sacks in all the other changing rooms and committed my own letter to memory as I sat down now, naked and quivering with growing apprehension, my hands in my lap in what was a laughably defensive pose.

'Right, I think I've got everything,' Anne-Marie

announced as she pushed open the door with the large plastic crate she was carrying. 'Here, budge up and let me put this down. This stuff is heavy.'

The *stuff* to which she referred was mostly rubber, which as any devotee of the fabric will tell you is indeed a dense material; even the flimsiest looking latex dress is surprisingly heavy when weighed in the hands. As I peered down into the box I saw that none of this looked at all flimsy and the first stocking that Anne-Marie passed to me felt as heavy as any boot I had ever worn.

'You'll need this,' she said, passing me a small tin. I saw that it was talcum powder, unscented according to the label. 'Everything is properly washed and then pre-powdered before being put back into wardrobe,' she went on, 'but I find it pays to just sprinkle a bit of talc on anyway and rub it over. That way the rubber slides on like it's oiled. Lovely,' she added, winking at me.

It was, indeed, a feeling I've since come to agree can be lovely, and whilst rubber can be awfully hot and uncomfortable in the wrong circumstances, in the right circumstances it can be a very sensuous experience and there's something about being dressed in it that always makes me feel a bit special and very, very wicked.

Even with the added talcum, I found that putting on latex stockings was a skill that did not come easily the first time out and required a great deal of patience from me and no little help and advice from Anne-Marie, to whom rubber was plainly not a mystery. Eventually, when I had smoothed the second stocking up to the top of my thigh, she produced a corset of the same black colour but made of much thicker rubber. I peered at it and saw that it was moulded into an hourglass shape as extreme as anything I had ever worn, except perhaps that awful dog suit.

'Too much for you?' Anne-Marie asked me tentatively.

I swallowed hard but shook my head.

'It tightens with straps at the back, rather than laces, see?' She turned the garment around for my closer inspection. 'You just lift your arms up and leave the rest to me, okay?'

She had chosen well, at least as far as my natural measurements were concerned, for although the corset was a tight fit the bra cups lifted and supported my breasts beautifully, leaving just the top halves of my pale mounds and the merest glimpse of my dark aureoles showing. However, as I peered down I saw that each cup had a vertical zip running down the centre and understood that my nipples could easily be accessed by this means when the time came.

'Comfy?' Anne-Marie asked as she fastened the final buckle behind me.

'Not quite the word I'd have used,' I joked nervously, 'but yes, it's not bad, considering. Shall I do the suspender straps now?'

'No, I'll do them. There are four on each side and you won't be able to bend much, so you won't get the spacing right and that's most important. These things have to look right or else it's all a waste of time and effort.' As she bent to the task, I tested the corset and the restraints it imposed upon my body and found that she was right. The thick rubber, although basically pliant, had been moulded in such a fashion that it formed an all but rigid carcass about me and bending was now all but impossible. I was also beginning to feel as if the top half of my body was separate from the lower half, there being little sensation of connection or support of the latter to the former.

'This must have cost a fortune,' I murmured, running two fingers down the sleek surface. 'What sort of place makes and sells these things?'

'Oh, more than you'd think, though of course it's not exactly what you'd expect to find in your local Marks and Spencer knickers department.'

I imagined my mum, who always bought her underwear from Marks and Spencer, and the expression on her face if she was ever confronted with something like this there, let alone if she saw it on her daughter.

'If you want, and if you like it that much, I can ask how much it is and you can take it home when we leave,' Anne-Marie offered, snapping another garter strap clip into place.

'Yes, okay,' I heard myself say and felt a thrill of guilt, not just at the thought of possessing such a piece of exotica but at spending the sort of money it surely cost. 'I suppose it can be worn with ordinary stockings?'

'Yes, but I'll sort out a couple of pairs of these. Your legs are so long, and they look lovely in latex, don't you think?'

'I can't really tell,' I said modestly, though I had to admit that my legs looked pretty good in anything, or in nothing at all, for that matter.

'Little Miss Rubber Lover,' Anne-Marie said, straightening up at last. 'No, don't deny it, I can see it in your eyes.'

'It's the smell,' I said, wrinkling my nose. 'There's something about it…'

'Yep, you either love it or you hate it, a bit like marmite,' she agreed, 'though I wouldn't want to try wearing marmite, not even in my kinkiest moments.' She turned away and delved into the box to produce a pair of high-heeled rubber ankle boots with thick platform soles.

'That's a bit much, surely,' I said, eyeing them and doing some rapid calculations. 'They'll make me around six-feet-six!'

'Six-eight,' Anne-Marie corrected me blithely. 'Nice and tall, which will make the slave image even more dramatic. People will be drooling over you.'

'The way Andrea drools over Carmen, you mean?'

'The way most people drool over Carmen.' She knelt down and began fitting the first boot to my foot, tightening the laces carefully. 'You know, Teenie, if you wanted to be a dominant you'd be a monster hit. Perhaps you should try it out with Andrea when we get back. She'd grovel at your feet if you told her to.'

'Well, originally I thought Andrea was more dom than sub and I thought the idea was that she did what you told her, not what I said.'

'Well, you're new to all this, so you'll learn. People often change roles back and forth, depending on who they're with and how the mood takes them at the time.'

'Can you be submissive?'

'Sometimes.' She looked up at me. 'Fancy having me as your slave for a weekend?'

'I… I don't know,' I stammered. 'Maybe… yes, maybe I would, but not just yet. I wouldn't know what to do or say.'

'Then you carry on being Teenie slave for a bit and you'll soon learn. Now, other foot, please.'

When she had finished with the second boot I found myself towering over her and feeling very uncertain. When I made to walk, I discovered it required more effort than I had expected for the thick soles seemed to drag behind me.

'They're weighted,' Anne-Marie explained, observing my consternation. 'Special slave boots to remind you that your pedestal is a punishment.'

'Oh, I see.' I made a face. 'My legs are going to be killing me if I have to walk in these for too long.'

'I don't think the idea is for you to spend that much time on your feet,' she said, and laughed softly, deep in her throat.

I felt that funny shiver again and wondered if I ought to change my mind about all this, but surely I had come too far now to retreat at such a late juncture.

The gloves required as much patience, expertise and additional talcum powder as had the stockings and I could not have put them on properly without help – not that first time, anyway. They were also black and seemed thin, but how tightly they embraced every knuckle joint left my hands feeling clumsy and alien. I held them up for closer inspection, flexing my fingers. To my surprise, I could only make a fist with the greatest effort and even then it was not a perfect one.

'Meg would have loved to have stuff like this to work with,' I mused, 'and so would that Pottinger bloke. I wonder when they first started making clothes like this?'

'Not that far back, at least I don't think it was. Rubber was for car and bike tyres, though they did start with incontinence pants quite a way back, now that I come to think of it. You should look it up as part of your history

116

studies.' Anne-Marie moved on now to buckle a high rubber collar about my neck, stretching up on tiptoe to reach properly. This collar was made of rubber as thick as that used for the corset, if not slightly thicker still, and it had been formed so it cupped beneath my chin and spread slightly onto my shoulders, forming a rigid support that now prevented me looking down or even turning my head. 'It's called a posture collar,' she explained. 'I like my slaves to hold their heads proudly when they walk. If I want their heads down then they get onto their knees, as I think you ought to do now... so I can fix your mask, silly,' she added, smiling at my surprised look.

It was easier said than done but I managed it with her holding one of my hands to steady me. She turned back to the box again but instead of the expected mask she now took out a length of chain with a square looking attachment at each end. She passed this about my waist and I saw that the two end pieces were designed to fit one inside the other with a dull click that told me they had been locked together, holding the chain snugly about my constricted waist like a belt.

'Right wrist please, Teenie.'

Obediently, I held up my arm and a shining steel band was clicked about it. My left arm was dealt with in the same fashion and then both were guided to my sides, where I discovered that each band was fitted with a small snap catch on the inside of the wrist that locked neatly onto the belt chain. Very simple and a pretty contrast against the black rubber, and also very effective in that I was now completely helpless.

'Now you're mine again,' Anne-Marie whispered, bending over to kiss me full on the lips, her tongue pushing between my teeth like an eager serpent. I wanted to reach up to hold her but my automatic response was halted with a clinking of metal as I tugged against it. 'Yes, all mine, my Teenie baby,' she said, breaking away from me, 'and don't think this is going to be just for a couple of hours. We can stay here for days on end if we choose to… if *I* choose to, I should say.'

'But what about the records we still have to check?' I protested. 'And what about Andrea?'

'Carmen will keep Andrea safe and sound and those records will still be there the day after tomorrow. After all, they've been there for decades already so another twenty-four hours won't hurt, will it?'

'You're not serious, are you?' I asked, feeling myself starting to tremble.

Anne-Marie stood back, her hands on her hips in a pose I had come to regard as Meg's. 'Perhaps,' she said softly. 'It all depends on how I feel and on how you perform.'

'Perform? What do you mean?'

'Out there,' she replied simply. 'It all depends how you act as my slave and how things go from there. Besides, you may not want it to end, not if the other night was anything to go by.'

'What do you mean?'

'Only that I think you're a natural little sub and a right little show off, given the proper conditions and preparation. In a few minutes you'll be masked and anonymous again and, once I'm changed, I'll be taking you out there just the way you are now, that's without panties, so your smooth little minny will be the centre of attention and available to all eyes and hands.'

'But I'm supposed to be *your* slave,' I protested. 'You

can't let just anyone—'

'My *slave*, exactly,' she cut in, 'which means that if I choose to let everyone touch you up, that's my privilege. Of course, there *is* a gusset piece I could put on you, I have it here in the box, but there's a downside to it.'

'Please use it,' I begged. 'Please cover me up.'

'Well, you asked for it.' She drew the thing out and I gaped as I saw the two attached rubber phalluses, the one slightly longer and thicker than the other but the second nonetheless imposing for all that.

'Oh, no!' I gasped. 'The other one, can't you take it off? I can handle the first one, but—'

'But you'll get used to the other one, I promise, and then you'll be reminded at every step that you're my slave girl by choice tonight.'

'But I think maybe I've changed my mind about that,' I said. 'Yes, I want to go.'

'Too late, Teenie slave. Besides, I don't think you really want to go. Now, I'm going to plug your pussy and your bottom, then I'm going to gag your pretty mouth and put your mask on you, and in a little while I'm going to show you off to all my friends, so move your legs apart while I put a drop of something on this little one for you. I imagine you'll have enough lubrication for its big brother by now.'

I stood and waited in total darkness while Anne-Marie changed. My mask had been designed so that the eye openings could be zipped closed and a flap clipped down over them to shut out even the last chink of light. It was a curious sensation, the thick rubber helmet mask padded slightly over the ears to dull sound, as was that of my lips stretched around the stubby rubber penis gag that was

119

buckled to either side of the mouth opening.

Hear no evil. See no evil. Speak no evil.

But there was no way of controlling my thoughts as they went whirling back in a kaleidoscope of images that included Meg, Hacklebury, Erik, Anne-Marie and Andrea. I stood tall and erect and knew that I was a thoroughly wicked person as I yearned for my mistress to take me out and parade me for all eyes to gloat over. My bottom felt full, my vaginal muscles throbbed as they expanded and contracted about their rubber guest, and I knew I could have made myself come on the spot. I think Anne-Marie knew that, too.

'Easy there, Teenie,' I heard her say close to my ear. She had to be standing on the bench seat, I realised vaguely. 'Save it for later and I promise you'll come all you want to and with an appreciative audience to share your pleasure!'

'I say, she really is a magnificent looking specimen!' The fellow at the bar was dressed from head to toe in white leather studded with rhinestones. His face was dead white and his eyes heavily made-up, his receding hair obviously dyed jet-black. I estimated he had to be in his early thirties and he spoke with an accent that suggested Oxford or Cambridge. 'What do you call her?' he asked, unable to take his eyes off me despite the fact that Anne-Marie's generous bosom was all but falling out of a top that could have come straight out of Wonder Woman's wardrobe had it not been made of white rubber.

'I call her Teenie,' my mistress told him.

'Not that teeny though, is she? My, but she's a tall one and such lovely legs, too. Do you rent her out?'

120

I felt myself turn cold, but was that totally from dread?

'No, she's not for rent,' Anne-Marie assured him with a wan smile, 'though I do loan her to very special friends.' It was half true, I thought, remembering Andrea and the way Carmen had looked at me earlier.

We moved on, Anne-Marie holding a short chain leash that she had clipped to my belt and me following just behind her, my feet dragging in their heavy-soled boots.

This area of the club was certainly for the more serious; the costumes were more dramatic and in many cases more extreme, to the extent that one male slave, his head encased in an eyeless leather helmet and his arms caught up behind him in a leather sling affair, wore nothing more than a ring set into his foreskin from which a slender steel chain allowed his red leather-clad mistress to lead him.

Other slaves, males and female and those whose gender it was impossible to guess accurately beneath layers of rubber and metal restraints, either followed their masters and mistresses in helpless and often blind obedience or waited mutely wherever they had been left, sometimes with leash chains clipped to handily placed hooks, sometimes strapped tightly to steel pillars that rose from floor to ceiling at strategic intervals.

The music down at this level of the club was loud, pounding and insistent heavy metal interspersed with Bowie and Queen and tracks I guessed had oriental or eastern influences in them but which were otherwise foreign to me. I could smell joss sticks in the atmosphere, the sharp acridity helping to override the heavy odour of perspiration, rubber and leather, except the mask that clung to my face served to flavour my every intake of breath with its own smell of latex.

There was a dance floor area in front of a raised stage, and although most of the patrons seemed to have things on their mind other than dancing, three pretty blonde girls emerged from the crowd clad in white leather boots and white leather briefs, feathered ornaments attached to their nipples, cat-like white masks on their faces and their hands caught up into fists inside tightly laced mitts. They were clearly someone's slaves and now they danced together, writhing forward and backward, circling and slithering around each other and sliding down onto their hands and knees. It was an impressive performance and I guessed they had to be professional dancers so supple did they seem and so perfectly in time with each other and the music did they remain.

Anne-Marie guided me forward towards the pillar nearest the left side of the stage, right at the edge of the dance floor. I leaned my weight slightly back against it, grateful to have something solid in this otherwise vaporous world of sound, smell and shimmering sights.

'We'll watch from here,' she said, speaking close to my left ear. The boots she wore were as high as my own – though the soles were not weighted like mine, she assured me – and so now she was once again able to come close to the level of my face even though I still towered over her and all but the tallest males in the place. It made me feel even more conspicuous than ever, for heads turned everywhere we passed and I could feel as many eyes upon me now as there were on the three blonde dancers.

'Carmen has organised a very special addition to the cabaret,' Anne-Marie informed me. 'Keep your eyes on the stage and you'll get a perfect view.'

The two Indian troopers came for her just after first light, binding her wrists roughly behind her back and dragging her out across the dusty parade ground to where the two lines of European soldiers stood ramrod straight in their fine red uniforms.

The young officer turned as Indira was thrown to her knees, an amused half smile flickering across his otherwise bland features. She glanced up at him once and then lowered her brown eyes, closing them so that she did not have to gaze upon her own nakedness and especially at the welt-striped mounds of her heavy breasts.

'This is part of the cargo that will accompany us to India, lads,' the lieutenant said, his reedy tones piercing the early morning air. 'Apparently she belonged to some nabob, but she escaped and hid away with some silly English wench and thought she'd become a lady's maid.'

There was a murmur of amusement among the ranks.

'We've been charged with taking the little brown hussy back to where she rightfully belongs, where they'll probably hang her, if they've got any sense. Her kind are nothing but trouble and they insinuate themselves among the weakest people, spreading their dirty foreign ways. This one, for instance, doesn't like men, wouldn't you know?'

The murmur of amusement became a much louder titter.

'Stick your vile tongue out girl and show these men. Quickly now, or I'll have the sergeant put you up and flog you again.'

Reluctantly, Indira extended her tongue to reveal the tiny gemstone adorning it.

'See that?' the officer cried. 'That's your pagan for you, and no mistaking. But what do you reckon she likes to do with her little ruby, eh? Why, she likes to put it into

other women, would you believe?'

This time the soldiers laughed openly.

'Yes, this little heathen seeks to deprive us men of the love and respect of womankind. She used that little tongue of hers to deprave and corrupt a perfectly sweet and innocent English virgin, causing her to turn against her betrothed and all her family. Hanging's too good for her, I say!'

'Leave her with us for the day, sir,' came a voice from among the soldiers. 'We'll soon show her what she should be doing.'

'I dare say you shall, Corporal Barker, so I'll leave her in your charge. Just make sure she stays in one piece until we get to Bombay, otherwise it'll be you who gets put up for the flogging and I'll wield the cat myself, by God I will!'

Indira stared at the lines of men, the rough faces, the well-muscled bodies and the leering eyes. Better that they should hang her here and now, she thought, than subject her to what she knew she would suffer at the hands of these barbarians. The ship to India would take weeks, months even, and the voyage had yet to begin...

We didn't have long to wait. As the music began to fade, the lights over the dance floor dimmed and died and the stage lights came up. Then, from the wing nearest to our position, strode Carmen. She was clad now in a tight leopard-skin leotard, the long sleeves of which ended in claw-fingered gloves, and there was a tight shiny corselet belt about her waist that matched her spike-heeled calf-length boots. She was carrying a coiled whip, which suddenly snaked out over the heads of the three retreating

124

blonde dancers with a resounding crack. Then she turned to face the crowd and a microphone rose on a stand from the front of the stage apron.

'Ladies and gentleman, good evening and welcome to *Sanctum!*'

There was a round of cheering and applause and the crowd that had been ringing the perimeter of the dance floor began pressing forward onto it, eager to find a good vantage point. I felt bodies pushing against me but my height, plus the additional advantage of my boots, meant my view remained unobstructed.

'As you all know,' Carmen began, 'our cabaret tonight includes many of our usual favourites, including Bella Donna, Lady Martina, Sir George and his Prancing Ponies, and our favourite drag queen, Fanny Gaslight.'

There was another ragged cheer.

Carmen smiled benignly. 'As ever, of course, we are open to all amateur talent and I think I can promise you one or two treats for later on. However, I thought I would start the proceedings tonight with a little treat of my own, a delicious little morsel of a girl with that little added factor so many of you appreciate.'

A wave of laughter greeted this remark.

'So, I shall waste no more time and give you Andrea, our very own little cockette!'

This time the applause was thunderous even though no one knew what was coming, and cheers rose from the crowd as the new star was pushed forward from the wings.

Of course, I wasn't surprised that it was our Andrea who appeared, but I *was* totally unprepared for the way in which she had been gotten up for her stage debut. Her face was its usual self, only made-up a little heavier, the foundation a little paler to emphasise the contrasts of her eye shadow, mascara and lipstick. From the top down she had been dressed completely in white – what there was of her costume, that is – but whether it was now correct to refer to her as feminine was a matter for debate. I saw that her neck had been braced with a posture collar not dissimilar to my own save for the colour and for the fact that it was made of leather as opposed to thick rubber. Her torso, from her neck to a point just above her navel, was clad in a tight top of stretchy white fabric through which it was possible to see two very large and very realistic looking nipples outlined at the tips of two extravagantly full breasts. These breasts were thrust into even greater prominence because her arms had been laced together behind her back within a single glove of white leather, her elbows nearly touching, her shoulders drawn back into what must have been a very uncomfortable position.

From head to waist, including the glittering green jewel now adorning her navel, Andrea was her feminine self, however, from there on down – if one discounted the white stockings and suspenders and the thigh-high white boots with their mandatory spiked heels – she presented a different aspect altogether and one which had me staring at her, wide-eyed. Of course, I've seen and even used such restraints since, but this was my first encounter with such a piece of clothing-come-equipment, so I shall describe it to you as it appeared to me then. It comprised a belt, from the front of which descended a triangular piece of white leather into which, at a strategic height and position, had been cut a circular hole around the edge of which, held there by tiny straps, ran a thick chrome-plated steel ring. Somehow or other, Carmen had succeeded in getting Andrea's cock and balls out through this ring, a feat which at the time I could scarcely credit, though having since learned a little more of the secrets of the male anatomy I know it can be achieved with the correct manipulation, a certain degree of care and no little amount of skill and patience. The triangle's apex, which pointed downwards, of course, was then drawn tightly by means of an attached leather strap that ran back up between the thighs and buttocks to where it cinched to the back of the belt, holding the whole thing snugly against the lower abdomen. Then, below the front opening, there was another thin strap, which had been buckled about the top of poor Andrea's scrotum so her balls were cramped inside the sac to the extent that the hairless flesh actually gleamed. As if this were not enough, and in Carmen's eyes it plainly was not, Andrea's cock was then held upright against the leather by means of several additional straps buckled tightly at brief intervals, the fourth and highest strap being tightened just behind the bulbous purple head.

I now know that such a restraint can be employed in two ways. One way is to stretch the semi-flaccid shaft and tighten the straps severely, which holds it apparently rigid and makes a full erection, as such, impossible, the blood flow generally succeeding only in swelling the head and top inch or two above the last strap. The second method is to first coax the erection and then employ the straps afterwards. I know of one mistress nowadays who, once she has fitted the main restraint, administers a dose of Viagra, or something similar, to her slave and awaits the inevitable result before using the straps. The slave's erection thus lasts for hours and the restraint has to remain on until the effects of the medication wear off, for it is impossible to retract cock and balls through that ringed opening whilst the former remains engorged. Back in the nineteen seventies there were no reliable medications of that kind, but there were other aphrodisiacs in herbal form and the correct stimulation at relevant intervals was enough to ensure that the slave's organ remained in the desired condition. Carmen, it seemed, preferred this method for she reached down and cupped Andrea's ball sack in one hand, squeezing it gently, and I saw her victim's eyes roll back at the contact.

'As you can see,' Carmen went on once the audience had had several seconds to take in the scene, 'Andrea is a hot little slut, but we have her well under control now. This naughty little thing,' she reached down with one finger to stroke the dark head where it bulged above the last strap, 'causes her to do really wicked things, but we've made sure it's going to be taught a proper lesson. Andrea can now satisfy only the gentlemen of the house; the ladies will have to seek other pleasures, I fear. So, if we can have some gentlemen volunteers, our little lady of the cock here will demonstrate what she can do with her pretty mouth, won't you Andrea, dear?'

I saw Andrea nodding as much as the high collar would allow and the pink flush spreading beneath the pale white make-up of her cheeks. Yet despite the blush, I seriously suspected she was enjoying this.

The first volunteer was not slow in coming forward, a tall, well built fellow in his late twenties, as far as I could tell from his face beneath the half mask that covered the upper portion of his features. He was dressed in boots and a sort of leather skirt with a chainmesh singlet and he wore heavy gauntlets on his hands. He pulled at his belt and the skirt or kilt fell away to reveal a cock that had itself been strapped into a form of restraint, although the straps of this particular device ran only about the base of his shaft and the top of his scrotum and clearly presented no obstacle to his quickly growing erection.

'On your knees, pretty slut,' Carmen commanded over the speaker system.

Andrea obeyed, sinking carefully down.

'Now show Master Toby what a good girl you're determined to become.'

And show him Andrea did, along with about a hundred-and-fifty other people, by opening her mouth and sucking him greedily into it. Her head bobbed so vigorously back and forth that Toby reached out his gauntleted hands to slow her actions.

Carmen intervened. 'No hands, Toby,' she admonished him. 'Only willpower is allowed here tonight, and the clock is running.'

I understood then that this was to be a sort of competition. Any man who wanted Andrea to suck him had to try to last as long as possible, and in that respect Toby did not set a very good marker. Within less than a minute I saw his eyes squeeze shut and his shoulders and arms go rigid. Andrea did not hesitate for a second and I shuddered, partly with the thrill of it, but partly in horror, as she drained him dry before releasing him.

All around us the audience broke into clapping and cheering again, but I guessed that most of their appreciation was for Andrea rather than Toby. Curiously, despite her stringent bondage and apparent helplessness, she had turned Toby into the victim, as she would turn several more men over the next half hour, or so.

The winner was a lanky fellow with a shaven head and tattoos all over his arms and his bare chest. He wore only a leather thong and high-heeled thigh-high boots, but there was nothing feminine about him apart from the spiked heels. Rather, he reminded me of a cruel pirate and his self-control was amazing. The last of the competitors, he easily surpassed the previous record of approximately seven minutes and still showed no sign of coming. Eventually, the crowd joined in a slow hand clapping in time with Andrea's bobbing head, and goodness knows how long this would have gone on had not Carmen stepped forward, seized the tattooed arm and raised it aloft.

'The winner!' she cried into the microphone. 'Master Julius proves once again that he is a true master and now he can claim the prize, if he so wishes. Andrea, up on your feet, you darling little slut, and show Master Julius what he has won.'

As Julius pulled back, his glistening erection swaying impressively before him, Andrea lurched uncertainly up onto her feet and turned away from the audience, bending at the waist to present her backside for all to see. Her tight little cheeks were separated by the strap from the restraint and beneath them was visible the rounded flange base of a dildo that had been inside her all along.

Carmen reached out, unbuckled the strap and eased the rubber shaft out, tossing it disdainfully into the wings. Then she looked at Julius and grinned. 'Up to you,' she said invitingly. 'She'll be the tightest fuck you've had in a good while, I'll bet.'

Everyone seemed to find this comment very funny and I gathered from this that Julius had possibly never had another man, even one with Andrea's mostly feminine appeal, but if that was the case, he certainly was not about to allow it to put him off.

'Is she well lubricated?' I heard him ask over the sound system, and Carmen nodded. 'Then why the hell not?' he roared. A moment later he was forcing himself into Andrea, gripping her hips so she could not avoid him even if she wanted to. He penetrated her slowly, until he was fully sheathed inside her tight hole, and then, in an almost comic little dance, he moved her around so the audience could see her face. To my amazement Andrea's expression was ecstatic, and as Julius began pumping slowly in and out of her, I saw her eyes glaze over and her jaw slacken as her mouth feel open. Her strapped cock was bulging between the leather bands and I could detect a glistening of her juices in the tiny eye in the centre of the dark purple mushroom.

'Oh, she loves every minute of it,' I heard Anne-Marie whisper. 'Little exhibitionist that she is, she'll remember this for months to come and my strap-on will be a poor substitute after a real cock!'

I couldn't tell whether or not Andrea was trying to fight the inevitable in an effort to spin it out but if she was, her efforts were a notable failure. Only a few moments later she came, the creamy liquid spurting two or three feet and much of it splashing back onto her while some of it sprayed the front row of the audience in a quite spectacular display. Sensing rather than seeing this, Julius joined her, and a yell of triumph from him accompanied by a shriek from Andrea signified that his own ejaculation was by no means any less formidable.

'Well, she'll be a bit subdued after that little performance,' Anne-Marie said, turning away and grasping my arm so that I followed her, 'but I doubt it'll last. Give her half an hour and she'll be ready for just about anything, our little star turn that she is!'

We stayed for a few hours but not, as Anne-Marie had threatened earlier, right through until the following day or evening. It was just as well, for although I did little more than follow her about as she mingled and chatted, the high-heels and the tight corset and collar became increasingly more uncomfortable as time passed. My feet, especially my toes, burned painfully, the backs of my legs ached, and by now I was growing thirsty, a problem which my gagged mouth prevented me from communicating to my mistress for the evening.

I was much admired by all. My height, and the posture that my outfit imposed upon me, made me the object of great interest and many comments were made on how this person and that person would love to borrow me, male and female alike. I half expected that at any moment Anne-Marie might accede to one of these requests, but she simply smiled and made little jokes that diverted her listeners from the subject.

Eventually, however, when Carmen joined us with a leashed and very subdued looking Andrea trotting obediently behind her, Anne-Marie decided that perhaps I should experience something myself. I looked down at Andrea, surprised to see that her male organ was once again as hard as ever, and wondered what was going through her head as she stared up at me.

'Andrea's tongue is as useful on females as it is on cocks,' Anne-Marie declared, and immediately the people around us in the bar area began to retreat, forming a tight little circle in which we were the centre of attention. My mistress then turned me around, unbuckled the back strap of the gusset and allowed it to fall forward between my legs. Immediately, the butt-plugging dildo began to slip out from inside me and there was nothing I could do to prevent its exit. The main dildo, however, remained firmly lodged within me even after Anne-Marie unbuckled the front of the strap and passed it to someone behind her. She looked up into my eyes and I stared back at her, silent and anonymous behind my mask and gag, my head held proudly erect by the stiff collar.

'I want to see you come, Teenie dear,' she said softly, 'and so do all these other people. I know you've been near to it most of the evening so it shouldn't take you long, but I'm going to make sure Andrea has you weak in the knees before she stops and then, I think, we'll let her actually fuck you.'

And so I found myself the centre of attention as Andrea stepped forward and knelt in front of me, reaching out to grasp the flanged base of my dildo between her teeth to pull its glistening black length slowly out of me. A hand reached out to take it from her and she began working on me with her lips and tongue, sucking and licking until she had coaxed my clitoris into proud attention, by which time I was already well into a continuous orgasm pattern. Only support from strong hands at my back kept me upright and I heard myself moaning through my gag as that wicked mouth and rough little tongue worked remorselessly on.

'Enough!' I heard Anne-Marie cry. 'Get those straps undone and then Andrea can finish her off properly.

I could barely see by this time and I had lost all sense of direction and perspective, but I knew well enough when that hard knob began to thrust inside me. I looked down, unable to believe Andrea could have managed this while my boots held me at such an impossible height. I learned afterwards that a small box had been pushed forward and that she had been helped up onto it in order to equalise our difference in heights, but at the moment it seemed like a miracle, like she must be floating just as I felt myself floating. I was so lost in my surrender that I barely felt her coming inside me. Even after she had pulled out I continued to shudder and buck, trembling and moaning as my climaxes went on and on and on…

Chapter Six

'How are you feeling?'

I was in my hotel bed, my eyes heavy from sleep, barely yet awake even though the sun was streaming in through the windows and I knew it had to be afternoon by now. I yawned and looked up at Anne-Marie where she stood beside the bed, a cup of something I guessed was coffee in her hands. 'I ache,' I said flatly. 'I ache and I'm tired and I think I ought to hate myself, and you.'

'And do you?'

'No, I don't think so. I ought to, though.'

'What makes you think that?'

'I would have thought that was obvious.' I struggled up into a sitting position. 'All *that*, last night...'

'That wasn't you, though,' she said, passing me the cup. It was coffee, hot and sweet. 'That was no more you than it was you back with Meg and company.'

'But it *was* my body this time,' I pointed out and sipped at the coffee, burning my tongue.

'No, it was *my* body,' Anne-Marie said bluntly. 'You surrendered it to me and I enslaved it, which means you can't accept blame or responsibility for anything that happened after that. Hate me, by all means, but don't hate or blame yourself.'

'Sounds like an easy way out, if you ask me,' I muttered.

'It is, and I'm not,' she retorted. 'Now drink your

coffee, have a shower and let's go and get something to eat. We've lost the morning, but we can still get a couple of hours more research in.'

When Andrea appeared in the foyer, I found myself wondering just how she managed it. Dressed in a cream two-piece outfit, albeit with her usual too-short-to-be-decent skirt, she looked smart, fresh, feminine and alert. She had not joined us for the late lunch Anne-Marie and I had shared in the hotel restaurant, but this was not on account of any diet. She ate much earlier, she assured us, and had even been out for an hour looking around the shops.

The taxi delivered us to our destination within a few minutes and we returned to our studies, but now it was slower work for we had to delve back through old copies of parish records, many of which were incomplete and, in some cases, missing completely. However, piece-by-piece, we managed to construct the outline of a family tree and gradually began to get some idea of the history of both the Hackleburys and the Carpenters, although we came no closer to discovering Gregory Hacklebury's final fate.

The original Hacklebury family had come down from the north from three villages around the Manchester and Liverpool areas, Daisy Hacklebury's brother moving south with his own family after her husband purchased Great Marlins. From tax returns, it appeared he had taken up the position of estate manager, but Gregory himself disappeared from the scene early on and only reappeared much later after Saul Carpenter's death with his freshly purchased title under his belt. As to whether he brought

Megan with him or not, we had no idea, but Andrea, setting off on her own line of investigation, came up with a startling piece of information. One George Crowthorne had worked for Saul Carpenter as assistant to his brother-in-law, and a further check of the records revealed that Megan Crowthorne had been born eighteen months after George's arrival on the estate, her mother, also named Megan, dying in childbirth.

'What are the odds that Saul was actually her father?' Andrea asked.

I pursed my lips. 'There's nothing there to suggest it,' I answered.

'No, but it might explain a few things about mad Meg,' Andrea suggested. 'If she was Saul's daughter, then maybe she thought she ought to have some claim to the place.'

'It wouldn't hold up,' I said. 'Apart from being female, even though there were no sons to dispute title, she was illegitimate, and whilst a male bastard might possibly have had some claim worth chasing, even that would have been dodgy. As a girl born on the wrong side of the blanket, she would have expected nothing.'

'Maybe not legally, but she obviously expected *something* judging from what you've told us about her.'

It was a good point and would certainly have gone some way towards explaining the curious relationship between Greg Hacklebury and his supposed maid, but there had to be more than that – we just didn't know what it was.

What we did know was that the estate would have passed to Daisy Carpenter upon her husband's death, probably with a bequest in there somewhere for the surviving daughter, Ruth, and possibly also with something in there for Gregory, who appeared to have taken over for his father when the older Hacklebury was killed in some sort of brawl with footpads, a fact we learned from a newspaper cutting Anne-Marie found just before we called it a day.

'Funny sort of crowd,' Andrea remarked. 'People coming and going and dying all about.'

'Life was a lot riskier back then,' I reminded her. 'No telephones, bad roads, and the railway still covering only the main routes. Somewhere like the area around Great Marlins would have been a different planet from the big cities, and there were always thieves and muggers on the roads.'

'And nasty bastards like Gregory running their own little empires,' Anne-Marie added. 'Poor little Angelina had no chance, did she?'

'Well, we still don't know what happened to her,' I said. 'Funny we can't find any record of her death.'

'Maybe she moved away or went abroad,' Andrea suggested.

'Or maybe Hacklebury or Meg killed her and *claimed* she'd gone abroad,' I reasoned darkly. 'And maybe there's only one way to find out.'

'No, you can't!' Anne-Marie exclaimed. 'Not yet, not until we know. If you go back there and they kill her... well, we still don't know what would become of you. There's no need, anyway. All this stuff happened well over a century ago, so nothing you could possibly do is going to change any of it.'

'Not so far as we know,' I agreed, 'but then we know squat about how all this works, and I reckon I was sent back there for a reason. I can't believe finding that locket and all those clothes wasn't meant to happen in some way. I mean, even inheriting the cottage was a bolt out of the blue.'

'That's because you're the only surviving female relative,' Anne-Marie reminded me. 'That wasn't fate, just your good luck.'

'Wasn't it? What do we know about fate and how it works?' I insisted.

'We don't even know if there *is* such a thing as fate.' Andrea looked back to where the spinsterish assistant curator was pointedly making a show of clearing her counter. 'But I reckon it's about time we were going now.'

'No clubs tonight,' I said firmly as we gathered our notebooks and pens. 'I want an early night and an early start in the morning and then, when we've finished here, I want to go back down to Dorset and see if we can't find out what's left of Great Marlins. I also want to see if anyone around there can recall any old stories that might help us get to the bottom of all this.'

We may not have gone clubbing that evening but we did not get the early night I had originally hoped for and it was probably lucky the hotel had thick walls, otherwise there would have been others who didn't get to sleep until late and we may well have found ourselves out on the street before midnight.

I should have guessed what was going to happen when we retreated upstairs after dinner. Lying on my bed was the black rubber corset, stockings, collar, gloves and boots from the night before, all polished and gleaming as they had been when I first saw them.

'My little present to you,' Anne-Marie told me, smiling

at the look on my face.

I realised she must have nipped upstairs during the time she had said she needed to pop to the toilet during the meal, and spread everything out for my return. 'They must have cost a small fortune,' I protested.

She patted my hand gently. 'You're worth it and you deserve it,' she said quietly. 'Besides, I just got a small bonus from my trust fund last week so I'm not short of a bob or two at the moment. And I also bought your cute little outfit,' she said, turning to Andrea. 'Your cock looked so sweet in all those straps, I couldn't bear the thought of waiting to see it like that again.'

'Not tonight, surely?' Andrea gasped.

'And why not? I think you should wear it all night and then you can share a bed with the two of us safely.'

'But I thought—'

'Nothing too strenuous,' Anne-Marie waved my protest away airily. 'Just a nice little costume cuddle-up with my two favourite girls.' Which was a bit like believing Hitler if he said he just wanted a little stroll across the border, but Anne-Marie had this way about her that just seemed to convince everyone she was right. Very soon I found myself once more in the role of Teenie the Slave, with a sullen looking Andrea once again strapped and restrained, only this time with a complicated harness holding a gag similar to mine firmly in her mouth.

Anne-Marie herself wore a red rubber cat suit with high-heeled ankle boots and gloves, but it seemed she was not intending to play an active role in the proceedings, at least not just yet. Instead, she unclipped my wrists from either side of my chain belt and pointed to Andrea. 'See if you can make her come,' she instructed. 'Just stroke her balls and what you can see of her cock but don't worry about her nipples. They're falsies, as you know. They may look impressive but she can't feel a thing through them. I tell you, Andrea, we ought to think about getting you real tits; you don't know what you're missing.'

With my hands free again, I suppose I could have removed my gag easily enough and protested that I would rather go to sleep, but the truth is that the sight of Andrea in all her white leather restraints was a huge turn-on for me and I wanted to see just how well I could control her for a change, having twice now been helpless at her hands.

I beckoned for her to come closer and this she did, lowering her eyes. Hesitantly, I extended one arm and carefully cupped her glistening sac in my rubber-gloved hand. I heard a sharp hiss from behind her gag and felt a tremor run down through her body. So far so good, but would she fight against it, or go with it?

I squatted down, wishing I had my tongue free, for that dark purple plum was just asking to be licked. Instead, I managed to work one latex-covered finger in past my gag, wetting it with my saliva. I withdrew it and carefully transferred the spittle to Andrea's cock-head, massaging it around until it gleamed with my wetness. My reward was a further groan from her stuffed mouth and an even greater swelling of the imprisoned shaft. I shuddered myself imagining how painful it must be growing for my poor victim, but I knew I was expected to continue until I had finished what I had started.

Inside me the two dildos suddenly seemed to have grown larger, as if in sympathy with the tethered flesh-and-blood version I was now tormenting. I stroked again, cupping and squeezing with my other hand, and Andrea began to whimper. I hesitated again, looking up in some alarm, but Anne-Marie urged me on.

'She's perfectly okay,' she whispered. 'Just suffering the most delightful torture of all. Take your time and don't rush it. Let her suffer as long as possible. She takes some bringing off, as you know, but all this might be a bit much for her, so go easy and make it last.'

It was a more than surreal situation, one almost helpless slave torturing a completely helpless slave to the very verge of erotic madness, or so it seemed. Andrea's feet began to move, performing a slow dance in time to my stroking and squeezing, yet not once did she make as if to pull away from me. She groaned softly, little mewling sounds like those of a trapped kitten squeezing past her gag. On what I could see of her strapped shaft, the veins bulged a dark blue, the thin leather bands seemingly about to cut through that tender flesh.

'Perhaps you should fuck her now,' Anne-Marie whispered. 'You've both earned it. You take your belt off and I'll loosen her straps. Better I do that in case you pinch her too hard.'

My two dildos slid out as one, dropping onto the carpet between my boots with soft thuds that should have had me cringing with embarrassment, but all I could focus on now was the cock that was being prepared for me. With each strap that was removed it seemed to grow bigger and bigger until only the scrotal strap remained, as had been the case the previous evening.

Anne-Marie turned back to check that I was ready, and then stepped aside. 'She's all yours, Teenie,' she smiled. 'Do your worst.'

Still gagged, I could only gesture or push and this I

now did, guiding Andrea back until she was against the bed and then pressing her against it, first to sit and then to lie stretched out on her bound arms, probably a most uncomfortable position, although I could tell she was now past caring about such things. Thanks to the ball strap her cock jutted conveniently upright and I lost no time in drawing myself up, my knees straddling her so I could poise my already soaking quim over it. I lowered myself onto the bulbous head, letting it press against my opening as I rocked back and forth a little, teasing her and making her wait for the moment of ultimate possession. Then suddenly I felt the rounded tip slip inside me as she strove desperately to push up into me. Only for a second did I consider rising up to continue the deprivation before I let myself sink, devouring every inch of her erection in one swift killing dive, crushing my buttocks hard against her outspread thighs and bringing forth a choked scream of sheer ecstasy from behind her gag.

'Fuck her slowly, Teenie,' I heard from behind me. 'Make her wait and draw everything from her. She'd do the same to you and no doubt will before long… that's it, my two sweet little girl slaves. Yes, that's perfect!' I saw the flash and realised dimly that Anne-Marie was now photographing this curious scenario, but I did not care. For one thing, I was unrecognisable in this outfit, and for another more important reason, I could not have stopped now had I wanted to…

And so it was eventually back to Dorset, this time deeper into the county and to the village of Marlin Cross, really no more than a hamlet comprising seven or eight cottages, a garage that looked as if it had been closed for a decade or more and a pub that had been closed for even longer, its faded paintwork and boarded windows witness to a diversion of the former main road that had left it high and dry.

'Not very promising,' Andrea observed, stating the obvious. 'No sign of the Carpenter empire here.'

We had discovered during our final sortie into Somerset House and another visit to the British Museum that Saul Carpenter had almost certainly been born Saul Carpentier, son of a French aristocrat of Jewish descent, the family having fled to England to escape the terror and afterwards changed their name to the English spelling. Beyond that, however, we were no wiser than we had been before.

'Looking at these buildings,' I said as I leaned back against the side of the car and stared up at the crumbling pub façade, 'I'd guess they were probably built after eighteen thirty-nine. The style is mid-Victorian, probably between eighteen sixty and eighteen ninety, although those two end cottages at the bottom of the street are probably a bit older.'

'You do know your history,' Anne-Marie complimented me. 'They all just look old to me.'

'You can tell from the windows,' I explained. 'These are much later, but the two buildings down there may well have been built as early as the mid-eighteenth century. Possibly estate workers cottages; they're about the right size.'

'Except there's no estate left any more,' Andrea observed, 'so what's the point of hanging here now?'

'There's a larger village about two miles further on,' I said, consulting the AA map, 'Minsley Hampton. It looks more promising. The main road comes back around and goes right through it, so presumably there'll at least be a pub there still.'

'Oh, alcohol!' Andrea sighed. 'And food! Please!'

There *was* a pub with alcohol and a selection of pies and pasties, if little else. There were also several dozen cottages, a couple of larger houses, a post office and a general store manned by two elderly looking females who simply had to be sisters.

'Remember,' I said as we sat in the farthest corner of the bar nursing large vodkas and lemonade, 'we're here researching for a film company that specialises in period dramas for television and my name is Teena Brown, just in case there's a Spigwell or a Thyme connection hereabouts.'

'If I was related to any of these,' Andrea looked down the length of the room to where four very rural types were propping up the far end of the bar, 'I wouldn't like to own up to it. This is the sort of place where they've only just stopped eating their children and a virgin is a girl that can run faster than her brothers!'

'Shut up, you daft bitch!' Anne-Marie hissed. 'We need cooperation here, not you putting people's backs up before we even get going.'

We left Andrea at the table with strict instructions not to move. Two of the men at the bar were already casting covert glances in her direction and not because they suspected her true gender. Again that skirt length of hers was drawing the wrong sort of attention.

We introduced ourselves to the landlord, a cheery enough individual who told us his name was Norman Bartwell, and he became even cheerier when we mentioned our fictitious film company and the possibility of location shooting in the area. You could almost hear the sound of cash registers jingling in his head as he conjured up images of a thirsty film crew and countless extras invading his pub, which would have become large enough to water a small army.

'Great Marlins, you say,' he repeated, scratching his stubbly chin. 'Yes, I've certainly heard of it, though it ain't been around in my time here and I've had this place, and my dad before me, for nigh on fifty years now. There was a Marlin House, of course. The War Office, or someone, used it during the forties, but Jerry must have found out about it and they snuck in and bombed him one night in forty-two... or was it forty-three?'

'And whereabouts was that?' I prompted.

Norman scratched his chin again. 'Well, you'd want to go back down the road about a mile-and-a-half and turn off up Vole Hill Road on the left. Then, about a quarter of a mile up, you'd want to be making a right and then another left near the top of the hill, and then follow the road down until you get to the stream, or what's left of it. You'll see some woods there and the house was behind them, but there's nothing left of it now. They took away the rubble to fill bomb craters on the Brimley aerodrome just before D-Day.'

'Who lived at the house before the army people took it over?' I asked.

'Old feller by the name of Spreadwell, or something like that.'

'Could it have been Spigwell?' My pulse suddenly picked up a gear.

Norman considered this. 'Might've been,' he conceded,

'but then again, might not. It was a long time ago, and I wasn't more'n a young lad. Funny bloke he was, though, bit of a hermit. Hardly ever came into the village.'

'Was there an estate there in his time?' Anne-Marie enquired.

Norman shook his head emphatically. 'No, definitely not, it was all farms across from Meg's Mount to Sprigley Cross, all except for a stretch along by the old river course that was flooded and marshy.'

'Meg's Mount?' Again my heartbeat picked up speed. 'Where's that? I haven't seen it marked on any maps.'

'Oh, bless you, my dear, and neither will you,' Norman laughed, 'not on any official maps, any ways. No, you'll see it on the ordnance maps as Filton Hill, but people hereabouts always calls it Meg's Mount.'

'Do you have any idea why?'

'Well, it's only an old tale, but there was a story that there was once a witch lived hereabouts and she used to sit naked on the big white ridge of rock at the top of the hill whenever there was a full moon. Folks said she used to ride it like it was a stallion.'

'And her name was Meg, was it?' asked Andrea, who despite our threats had now wandered up to the bar in time to catch these last exchanges.

'Well now, young miss,' Norman replied, his eyes twinkling, 'if she'd been called Lizzie, then I reckon the place would've been known as Lizzie's Mount, don't you?'

We all laughed at that, all except Andrea, who had decided it was time for a good sulk. We ordered her another drink and pressed on with our host.

'Who else might know some of the old stories?' I continued our friendly interrogation.

147

'Old Jacob Henley, I reckon,' Norman replied. 'He's in his nineties and is the oldest person in these parts except for old mother Redford, who lives with her granddaughter and can't even remember her own name, so I doubt she'd be of much use to you.'

'And where might we find Mr Henley?'

He grinned. 'You can find him right here at about six o'clock when we reopen. Never missing, never late. He lives just up the hill, but I wouldn't go knocking on his door at this time of day. He likes to nap for a bit in the afternoons and he gets right crotchety if anyone disturbs him. No, you come back after six if you can and I'll introduce you proper, like. Mind you,' he added, 'better have the price of a couple of pints of Old Oakleys with you, for him, I means. Old Jacob always reckons everything has to have a price, and that's usually it.'

'This would be quite exciting,' Anne-Marie said, 'like a treasure hunt, only there's no treasure we know of and we don't even know what we're looking for anyway.'

'I'll know it when we find it,' I muttered as she pulled the car into a muddy track entrance at the side of a road that was scarcely any wider. I opened the door, climbed out and sniffed at the air. 'We're close, I know we are,' I said. 'I can feel something.'

'Like a tingling in your bones?' Anne-Marie said mischievously, smiling.

'A feeling in her waters, as my granny used to say.' Andrea swung her legs inelegantly out of the rear door and swore as she snagged a stocking on it. 'Fuck it!' she growled, her voice dropping an octave. 'These were new on this morning. And why do I always have to sit in the

148

backseat anyway?'

'It's just a sort of sense,' I added vaguely, ignoring her outburst as I walked a few yards along what remained of an old hedgerow and found a place where I could climb up to look across to where the woods began. It was a poor sort of coppice, nothing like the grand acreage I had been walked around at Great Marlins, but it was one of the few growths of trees that went on for as far as the eye could see in every direction. 'It's definitely the place,' I said firmly. 'But why doesn't it show up on any of the maps we looked at?'

'People made mistakes years ago same as they do now,' Anne-Marie said, 'and if it was bombed out during the war, the mistake wouldn't have been worth correcting, would it?'

'That must be Meg's Mount over there,' I said, pointing away to the east to where a hill rose up, its crest gleaming white in the late afternoon sun at one end of the ridge. 'It's close enough to have been part of the old estate, though I never saw it when I was back here.'

'The place was all woods then,' Anne-Marie reminded me, 'so you wouldn't have been able to see very far. Which way do you want to go first? I don't fancy trying the car up this track. The mud's as hard as iron and I can't afford to lose my suspension.'

'Let's walk,' I decided. 'I need to see what's left of the old house. Maybe I'll recognise something.'

'And maybe you won't,' Andrea snapped, 'or did you write your name on a special brick?'

We both pointedly ignored her and set off, carefully picking our way over the hard mud ridges. Progress was slow but at least it was progress, which is more than would have been possible had it rained in the past few days. And as we gradually approached the trees, I felt a curious tingling in my spine that told me we were on the right track, though to what, where, and for why, I still had no real idea.

In many ways, the site of the old house was a complete disappointment, for whatever the repair men from the RAF base had left behind during nineteen forty-four had long since become overgrown. Yet with every step we had taken towards the woods, that feeling of mine had become stronger and stronger, so that when I finally stood where the house had once been, an area where the trees had not yet encroached, I knew this was indeed the place.

'There's a funny smell everywhere,' Andrea said, sniffing.

'That's mint, I think,' Anne-Marie hazarded a guess. 'It grows wild near nettles and dock leaves and there's plenty of both of those around here, so watch your legs and fingers if you don't want to get stung. This is a right wilderness.'

'It is,' I agreed, 'but you can see from the different growth where the foundations must be. See that line of scrubby little stuff along there, that must have been... the front wall, I reckon, because it's facing south and most houses were built facing south in the old days.' I walked across to the line I had spotted and stooped down, making sure there were no nettles before I started tugging at the straggly growth. 'Yes, here you are!' I cried. 'Look, bricks just at ground level, or where ground level would have been. This is the old foundation, all right.'

'Terrific.' Andrea folded her arms across her chest.

'We've come all this way to see a line of buried bricks. If I'd known that, I could have buried a few new ones in our garden for you.'

I looked up at her, frowning. 'What's the matter with you today?' I demanded. 'There's no talking to you, is there?'

She made a face, and turned away.

'She's having a mood on because I'm punishing her for being a right selfish little bitch,' Anne-Marie informed me. 'But if she thinks acting like this is going to do her any good, then she's got another thing coming.'

'Punishing her?' I echoed. 'How?'

'Show her, you sulky little tart,' Anne-Marie ordered.

Andrea hesitated, but then turned back towards us. We were all wearing jackets even though the weather was mild enough for us to keep them open, and Andrea reached down and grasped the hem of her skirt, raising it with a defiant pout.

'Ah, I see,' I said, and I certainly did, for beneath the slightly flared skirt she was wearing the white leather restraint that strapped her male organ tightly against her lower belly. 'Oh, poor you.'

'Yes, poor me,' she retorted, letting the skirt fall again. 'This thing is bloody uncomfortable and I can't even wear any knickers with it.'

'Then you should learn to act in a more considerate fashion.' Anne-Marie sounded less than sympathetic. 'All you've done these past few days is complain, other than when you've been getting what you want, so I've put you in that nice cock harness to remind you just who, and what, you are.'

'Well, I'm hardly likely to forget that now, but it's not

fair. This thing makes me feel randy as hell, you know, and there's not much chance of me getting any relief just now, is there?'

'Well then, why don't you do it yourself while we watch,' Anne-Marie suggested. 'That'll make for a pleasant diversion, won't it, Teenie?'

'Um, yes, I suppose so,' I agreed.

Andrea looked downcast. 'I can't,' she said. 'You know I can't. I've never been able to, have I?'

'Then maybe now's the time to start learning,' Anne-Marie said firmly. 'Poor little Andrea has never been able to wank herself off, you see,' she said to me by way of explanation. 'She either needs someone else to do it for her, or else she needs to fuck properly. She's been spoiled, if you ask me.'

'Well, maybe I could…' I began. I hated seeing Andrea so miserable and we certainly weren't going to get any sort of cooperation from her in this state.

'No,' Anne-Marie insisted with an air of finality, 'she can do it herself or she can stay all strapped up and randy until tomorrow. Go on, Andrea, take your skirt off and give us a show.'

'You're a wicked bitch!' Andrea wailed, but all the same began unfastening her waistband. 'You know this isn't going to work.'

'Shut up and do it,' Anne-Marie snapped. 'You can undo the top three straps, but the bottom one and the ball clincher stay where they are. You can do us a little dance first, if you like. Or shall I find a length of twig and whip your backside for you?'

'No, don't do that!' Andrea all but sobbed. 'I'll try, honestly I will, but it's not my fault!'

'Let her try,' Anne-Marie whispered to me as Andrea began tugging at the restraining buckles, 'and then I'll toss you to see which of us finishes the silly tart off. There's no way she'll come by herself, same as she says.'

It was actually me who lost, or won, depending upon your point of view, when we tossed the coin. Astonishingly, given that Andrea had spent a fruitless fifteen minutes trying to masturbate herself without any joy, it took only a few strokes from my hand to have her spurting forth like a fountain. Anne-Marie was all for leaving the restraint in place and re-buckling the other straps afterwards, but I prevailed upon her to relent and, after waiting a few minutes for Andrea's erection to finish subsiding, we left her to remove the device while we began walking away from the line I estimated was the rear of the old house.

'The place where they kept me was definitely at the back of the house and down a hill through the trees,' I said. 'Look, the ground slopes away here and there are still a few old trees, so this could be the way, though stuff will have grown and died all over the place since then.'

'How far was it?' Anne-Marie asked after we had walked a good ways and were already approaching the farther edge of the coppice.

'I'm not sure,' I admitted, 'but it was further than this, quite a bit further, in fact.' We walked on and came out into the open again. 'It's all so different,' I said. 'There was a path through the trees and we walked for quite a ways, but then... yes, the ground levelled out again and then it was about another two or three minutes...

somewhere over there,' I said, pointing across what was now an overgrown meadow boasting a few scrubby bushes.

'I wonder where all the trees went?' Anne-Marie mused out loud.

I shrugged. 'They were still building ships mostly from wood right up until eighteen sixty and even after that, for merchant ships, anyway. Maybe whoever was in the hot seat here sold off all the timber; it would have fetched a fair price.'

'Sounds like vandalism to me,' Anne-Marie said sourly. 'But then that's men and their wars for you.' She turned to me. 'Are you sure we're going the right way?'

'No,' I admitted, 'but I'm still getting a feeling, so let's move on a bit further.'

The best way to explain the way I felt as we continued walking might be to compare the tingly sensation I was experiencing with the clicks from a Geiger counter – the closer we came to where I knew we had to go, the faster and stronger grew the little electric tremors in the base of my skull and the tips of my fingers. And if we began to stray away from the line, the sensations began to dull. Eventually, several hundred yards from the site of the house, I stopped and squatted down on my haunches. 'Here,' I said simply, running my fingers through the long grass.

'Here what?'

'This is where that shed, stable, kennel, whatever you want to call it, was. It was right here, right where we're standing. The feeling is very strong here.'

'It just looks like flat ground to me.' Anne-Marie slowly turned three hundred-and-sixty degrees. 'Not even any 'sign of old foundations like there is up at the house.'

'They may not have put in any proper foundations,' I said, standing up again. 'It wasn't much of a building and only one storey, so they may just have built on the surface. The floor inside was only hard earth with straw on it and I got the feeling the place had been constructed in a bit of a hurry especially for me... for Angelina, that is.'

'Well, if this is the place, what now?'

'I don't know,' I admitted. 'This is definitely the place, but I don't know what comes next. I just knew I needed to come here, perhaps just to convince myself it really did exist and that it wasn't just a figment of my imagination.'

'And you're convinced now?'

'Yes.' I nodded emphatically and scraped at the earth with the toe of one shoe. 'Yes, now I'm sure, though why I should be convinced because of a tingly feeling, God only knows. The whole thing is... well, it's mad, and so is everything else that's happened to me since.'

'You mean me?' Anne-Marie asked quietly.

I looked at her and shrugged again. 'Well, I mean, think about it,' I said. 'A few weeks ago I was just an A-level schoolgirl leading a perfectly normal life with a perfectly normal family and perfectly normal friends. Now I've been back over a hundred years and... well, we both know what happened there, and when I get back here to nineteen seventy-five, we spend half our time playing kinky games with a boy who seems to want to be a girl except for the fact he's got a very active cock, and I end up being fucked in front of an audience of total strangers. I'm beginning to wonder if I might not have gone mad,' I said, running a hand through my hair. 'Maybe none of this is real, maybe this is all just a dream and I'm going to wake up somewhere in a straightjacket.'

'It's real enough,' Anne-Marie assured me, moving closer and gently taking my elbow. 'Poor Teenie,' she whispered. 'We've rushed things too much and not really thought about what must be going through your head. I'm a selfish bitch. I can't even begin to think what this must be like for you here and now, let alone when you went back in time.'

'To be honest, I'm not even sure how this is for me now myself,' I confessed. 'There's the tingly feeling, but otherwise I feel sort of numb. I don't know what I expected to find here, but it wasn't absolutely nothing, which is precisely all we *have* found.'

'We ought to look around a bit. Maybe we could still find something.'

'Oh, you mean like a discarded leather suit with a dog mask or maybe a whip with Meg's initials on it?' I asked sourly. 'No, we're not going to find anything here. During the war there would have been hundreds of service people wandering all over the place. If there were any little trophies or relics, they'd have found them. Besides, there wasn't much in the place to leave behind aside from a few buckets and the odd length of chain. Whoever knocked the place down would have taken everything away first.'

We turned around and began walking back up towards the site of the house, stopping when we emerged from between the trees again to turn and look across towards the crest that was Meg's Mount. The late sun still glinted along the chalky section, but now the white line was beginning to look distinctly orange.

'I wonder what *did* happen to her?' I was speaking as much to myself as to Anne-Marie. 'Did she end up going off her head and just wandering around the woods and hills? Something must have happened, because there's one thing we don't know.'

'And what's that, Teenie?'

'Well, we found that record of her registering her title to the estate, didn't we? But nowhere does there seem to be anything written down as to how the estate was sold or broken up. There are title deed records to all the farms around here now, or there ought to be, but nothing to show how Meg disposed of everything, the house included.'

'Maybe she didn't. Maybe she just died and went mad and this Spreadwell or Spigwell bloke was... well, maybe he was Angelina's son and he just stayed on here.'

'He'd have had to be bloody Methuselah then,' I replied. 'If he was a son of Angelina's, then that would have made him at least a hundred by the time the last war started.'

'Grandson then,' Anne-Marie persisted. 'Either way, I reckon he had to have been a Spigwell and not Spreadwell; the name's no coincidence.'

'No,' I agreed, 'I don't think it is. But whoever he was, and whatever his name was, I don't think it's important to me. But then again, same as I said, I don't know what is, or isn't, important any more.'

The four troopers were very drunk now and barely able to speak coherently, but the bearded corporal beckoned to Indira with an unmistakable gesture.

Slowly, she crawled across the bare floorboards to him and lowered her head. 'Master?' she whispered without looking at him. She could feel his lustful eyes boring into her, taking in her nudity and her heavy breasts with their gold nipple rings, which had been the object of great interest among these rough and ready men. They had been tugged and twisted as much as she herself had been beaten and continually abused, a plaything for these men who would go out to defend an empire from barbarism and yet who thought nothing of throwing a defenceless girl on her back and using her merely for their own satisfaction.

'Y'know what I want,' the corporal slurred, dropping the near empty bottle on the floor. 'Get yer arse over here and suck my bobbin, ya heathen slut.'

Indira slithered closer and reached into his lap to unfasten the waistband of his breeches. She had to delve deep to find his weapon, for it was limp and lifeless.

'Get to it, whore, make me bobbin stand up and then you suck him dry, else'n I'll ram me boot so far up yer cunt ye'll be able to polish the toe through yer mouth.'

Obediently, Indira took the flaccid organ in hand and began manipulating it. Somewhere behind her she heard a crash as a bottle hit the floor and shattered, followed by a muffled curse and then a groan. She risked a glance over her shoulder and was rewarded by the sight of two soldiers slumped unconscious against the wall. The third soldier was sitting cross-legged and swaying in a stupefied fashion.

She returned her attention to the corporal, for it would not do to stir his ire just now. He had whipped her twice already since the beginning of the week and took great pleasure from tying her hands and leaving her helpless and naked for hours on end, available for any man who ventured into the guard hut and took a fancy to her. Her deft fingers worked away... she needed her hands free, for escape would be impossible if he tied her up again.

The wall at the edge of the compound was not that high, but she would need her hands if she were to scale it...

'Whaddaya fuckin' about there?' the corporal peered blearily down at his organ, which had managed a half-hearted salute. 'Get the fucker in yer fuckin' mouth, ya he... heathen...' His head lolled forward and his fingers slackened around the bottle they had been nursing.

Indira grabbed at the glass neck before it could fall, moving it carefully aside and placing it quietly down on the floor. Her other hand remained wrapped around the corporal's cock, though it was no longer responding and would not now – not for a few hours, at least.

She peered back at the cross-legged trooper, the last of the four men still conscious, and then across the room to where the earlier discarded bottles lay haphazardly in a pile to one side of the wood stove. The man still rocked slowly back and forth, his eyelids drooping ever further, but somehow he seemed to be resisting the pull of sleep, fighting against both the alcohol and the herbal sedative Indira had added to each bottle she had opened for them.

What remained of the ground powder, no more than a few grains, was inside the corner pocket of the ragged smock dress that was all they had given her to wear. Not even a pinch of the powder was left from a handful she had managed to prepare when she was supposed to be cooking and no one was watching. It was surprising what grew wild in England and even along the walls and fences of an army barracks amidst dandelions and nettles and the first wild snowdrops of spring. All she had needed was a few leaves picked and left to dry at the back of the stove, then pressed into the palm and worked with determined knuckles until they were broken down into a *fine dust, which she had slipped into a few wine and rum bottles where the taste would be swamped by the sharp edge of the cheap liquor. It was only a mild dosage, and even taken in greater quantities the herb was not deadly, but it was enough to induce a deep sleep when mixed with alcohol, especially at the end of a long day. It was enough to keep her captors out of action for the time she needed to slip away through the darkness and get to that wall.*

'They shall not send me away from you, my cherished little jewel,' she whispered, turning back to check that the corporal was now completely unconscious. 'The evil one shall not harm you, shall not have you, even if I have to give my very life to make it so. This I swear by everything I hold sacred.' She closed her eyes but her lips continued moving in a silent incantation whilst behind her a soft thud told her the last man in the room had finally surrendered to the arms of Morpheus.

This time I had no sensation of passing out, no falling through space, no blackness, no nothing. One minute I was walking back up towards the site of the old house with Anne-Marie and the next I was laying in the straw back in that horrible little prison.

My arms and legs felt stiff, not just sore but completely stiff and useless from their rigid encasement within the leather suit, and my first attempt to rise proved useless, for without flexibility in either my knees or my elbows I was like a turtle pushed over onto its back, my limbs flailing uselessly in all directions.

I paused, forcing myself to lie still for a moment and consider the situation.

I remembered that Erik had lowered me bodily to the

floor earlier, but surely I was not stuck like this just because he was not here to help me? With a great effort I attempted to lift my upper body using only my stomach muscles, a feat I practiced regularly in the gym, but that had been in my own well-tempered body when I was not handicapped by the tightly laced corset that now compressed my middle.

I relaxed again and considered another option.

I spread my stiff arms wide and then around and above the level of my shoulders, pressing back down into the floor in an attempt to obtain some leverage, but this proved another failure.

I thought again.

This time, I placed my arms tightly against my sides and began to rock from back and forth, gathering momentum until I managed to roll completely over my right arm and onto my stomach. So far so good, I thought, or else I had just traded lying helplessly on my back for lying helplessly on my stomach, my padded muzzle pressing deep into the straw. Now for the tricky part…

I stretched my arms again, bringing them around so that they were above my head, and pressed the padded paw ends against the wall where it joined the floor, but nothing happened. I grunted with exasperation and would have cursed out loud had I been able to speak.

I thought some more, and got another idea.

I rocked myself over to the left and wedged my right paw hard against the wall, throwing my weight back again and likewise jamming my left paw against the unyielding surface. Success, at least a minor one, for my breasts were now held just clear of the floor even though the pressure on my arms was enormous. I quickly tried a repeat performance and was actually able to raise myself into a sort of press-up position. I tensed my muscles and concentrated on my legs, performing a kind of bunny hop that dragged my feet along in the direction of my hands. It was more than just hard work, but I repeated the move three or four more times until I was finally up on all fours, and from there it was simply a matter of straightening up into a standing position.

'Back down where you belong, bitch!'

I all but jumped out of my skin – both my skins – as I swung around to face the door and Meg, who stood on the threshold flexing what looked like a riding crop and smiling wickedly.

'I said get down like the dog-bitch you are!' she commanded, swishing the crop before her.

I could have cried, not so much from being made to resume my four-legged stance but from the knowledge that she had almost certainly been standing there, silently watching my near superhuman effort to get myself on my feet. I dropped my front paws to the floor and regarded her balefully.

'Much better.' She stepped forward and, taking hold of my collar, began leading me around the small room, chuckling and making nasty little comments all the while. Eventually she tired of this circular promenade and squatting down before me, she looked me straight in the eye. 'You can never hope to be a real wife now,' she whispered, 'not after this. Even if you were to wear the finest gowns and jewels, he would always look at you and see you as you were last night, my little bitch in heat. He'll see your doggie face and your gaping pussy beneath your lovely curling tail and that's how he'll want me to keep you. Then he'll grow tired of the game and I'll find him other amusements. You'll be my little doggie forever, here in your nice quiet kennel, and you'll have your pups and if one of them is right, then he'll be brought up as the son of the house, but he won't be right, so it will never happen. *I'll* give him the son he needs myself, my little Sheba. It'll be his son and mine and he'll be master of the Marlins one day and you'll be *his* pet dog. Ha, that'll be a fine day, though you'll be an old dog by then, I think. Old and sagging, with a cunt that's tired and loose.' She straightened up again.

I lowered my head. I had already known she was completely mad, but now I had seen something more than simple insanity in her eyes as she spoke of her plans for me. I'm not sure the words had ever been invented that could plumb the depths of what I felt towards Megan Crowthorne just then. I would go back to my own time, I *hoped* I would go back to my own time, but what of Angelina? My sanity was protected in some way by the temporary nature of my predicament, but whenever Angelina was back in her own body, she would not have that small luxury. When it was she who crouched here as Sheba, she would know she was facing a lifetime of this painful humiliation with the only release her eventual death.

I knew that in her place I should soon be praying for death, maybe even trying to help nature on its way, but then I was not Angelina, and neither, I resolved, would I leave her to suffer if there was any way I could put a stop to Meg. Easier said than done, however, for what hope is there for a dog girl? What can a person do when she is confined to all fours on stiff legs and arms with even her power of speech denied her?

But if there really was nothing I could do, why was I here? Surely I had not been brought back in time merely to witness and share in the suffering of one of my ancestors? There had to be more to it than that – the big question was *what?*

Erik arrived just as Meg was leaving. The two of them went outside together and I heard the sound of them conversing, though I could not make out what they were actually saying. Erik then returned alone and, using the metal funnel, gave me a drink of water before fastening my leash.

'Walk now we must,' he said, 'and necessary business you must be doing.'

I groaned inwardly for I could feel that I needed to do more than pee now despite the fact that I could not remember when I had last eaten any solid food. Perhaps Angelina's body had been fed during my absence from it since I didn't feel particularly hungry, but then having your stomach compressed as mine was now is not exactly conducive to a healthy appetite.

I shan't go into the details of what followed save to assure you that it was most embarrassing and, though you may find it hard to believe, far more of an ordeal in its way than being displayed the previous evening before Hacklebury's houseguests and then used by each of them in turn. At least I assumed it had been the previous evening, but I could easily have missed a day or two, or even more.

When we returned to my kennel stall, I saw that a bowl of some sort of oatmeal had been left on a stool, presumably by one of the maids, during our absence. I wondered if Erik might release me from the dog face mask in order that I might eat, for there was no way I could feed from the bowl in the manner of a real dog, but instead he used the same funnel that had earlier delivered the water to my throat to tip small quantities of the thin mixture into my mouth, allowing it to trickle down towards my throat. And with some difficulty, I managed to swallow it.

'Now to the house we are going,' he announced when the bowl was finally empty. 'Mistress Meg is saying that master himself you wanting there is.'

So, I thought as I lumbered awkwardly ahead of Erik back up the winding path, the bitch was determined to make sure Gregory got used to the idea of me as his pet dog, for I felt certain it was she and not he that had instigated this latest house call.

Sure enough, it was Meg who was waiting for us outside the kitchen entrance, the same crop in her hand and a smirk of triumph on her face as she watched my ungainly and humiliating approach. I saw she also held a tangle of straps in her left hand, which she now handed to Erik. 'Take her through into the library and prepare her as I instructed,' she said sternly. 'I'll be through in a few minutes to check your work.'

Erik nodded and moved ahead of me to lead the way through the passageways until we entered a long room lined on three sides with bookshelves and on the fourth by a series of high windows looking out upon a flat expanse of lawn. The shelving on the wall opposite these windows was broken up by a massive fireplace, which for the moment stood dark and empty, two unoccupied chairs on either side of it. Erik guided me to one of the chairs, but I was not to be permitted the luxury of sitting in such a human fashion. Instead, he stooped down and began adjusting the small straps at my knees that augmented the lacing on my legs, and I heard the slight rasping of buckles before he straightened up again.

'Bending the legs now you can and sitting down like good dog, please,' he said.

To my surprise, I found that I could indeed flex my knees now, though with some effort. Nevertheless, I persevered and was eventually able to sit back on my haunches as I had done once before in another suit, placing my supposed forelegs out in front of me.

Immediately, Erik bent over me again and I learned the purpose of the straps Meg had given him. One strap was buckled about each of my ankles and then the longer strap to which it was attached was passed about my thighs and tightened. In this way I was kept in my sitting position with no chance of rising until someone decided to undo the straps.

'A very nice picture, indeed,' Meg declared as she entered the room and walked down its length to where I sat. 'The faithful doggie waiting for her master, all prepared to keep him company while he works.'

And that was precisely how I passed the next few hours, my legs at first protesting with cramps and twinges but eventually growing completely numb. I knew I was in for agonies when I was finally permitted to stand upright again and I dreaded the moment, but first I had to endure the boredom. Do real dogs grow so bored just sitting there as I did whilst Gregory, with barely any acknowledgement of my presence, sat at the large oak table perusing countless documents? It seemed like an eternity before he finally sat back and, stretching, glanced over at me. Then he rose, slowly walked towards me, and dropped to one knee before me so our faces were level.

'She'll grow tired of this game before too long,' he said in a surprisingly sympathetic tone. 'Once she is sure you are no threat to us, then we can find you somewhere more comfortable to live and something a little more suitable to wear. Just be a good girl until then and try not to upset her.' He patted the top of my head.

I fought back an overwhelming urge to growl at him. I wished the metal strap across my tongue did not prevent me from doing more, for I wanted to shout at him and ask the bastard if he really thought his words should make me feel better. What the fuck was he? Was he, or was he not, supposed to be the master here? And why should anyone worry about upsetting a mere maid? Except, of course, that I knew she was more than just a servant. Whether she was Carpenter's illegitimate daughter, or whatever her relationship was either to Hacklebury, his aunt, his cousin or anyone else, Meg was definitely pulling most, if not all, of the strings around here. And if Gregory Hacklebury really thought Meg would tire of humiliating me and allow him to ensconce me in some quiet little room with a nice new wardrobe, then I was pretty damned sure he had another thing coming to him.

'Teenie! Teenie, are you all right?!'

I opened my eyes and saw Anne-Marie staring anxiously at my face. Looking around me, I realised we were still standing halfway between the site of my former imprisonment and the site of the house itself, where I could see Andrea waiting for us.

'Are you all right, Teenie?' she asked me again urgently.

I blinked a few times before I was able to find my voice. 'I... I think so,' I murmured, surprised to discover that I was standing. 'I went back there again, back in time, I mean. I was up at the house. Did I pass out?'

'Sort of, you went a deathly white and your eyes went blank. It only lasted for a few seconds or so, but it was quite spooky!'

'I didn't fall?'

'No, you just stood there the same as you're standing there now. How long were you back there for this time?'

'Not long, maybe a couple of hours, maybe three or four hours. No longer than that.' I shrugged against a breeze that was now beginning to feel decidedly cold. 'Come on,' I said, grabbing her hand, 'let's get back to the car. I could use a cup of tea before we go back and interview our ancient yokel.'

We drove back onto the main A35 road and then back towards Minsley Hampton and the pub, which was still closed for the afternoon. Four miles farther on we found another village with a café where we paid silly money for not very nice tea and slightly limp ham sandwiches, but at least the break warmed us up and occupied most of the rest of the afternoon and early evening, before it was finally time to drive back again and find Jacob Henley.

The pub could only have been open for two or three minutes by the time we arrived, but old Jacob was already there, as Norman our host had promised he would be. I introduced us, he happily accepted the offer of a pint of Old Oakley bitter, and then he was more than willing to talk. For a very old man, he had a surprisingly thick shock of white hair and very alert eyes. Whatever ravages time might have otherwise wrought upon his ninety-something-year-old body, it was obvious that his mind had survived as well as his thatch.

'Spigwell, yes, John Spigwell, he was. Yes, I knew him all right, insofar as any of us hereabouts ever knew him. He was like what you might be after calling a recluse, lived in that big house all on his own excepting for some woman who cooked and kept house for him. No, nothing like that, you understand, she was just paid help and lived in, but they must have been fair rattling around the place, just the two of them. She used to come into the village about twice a week for milk and flour and all the usual stuff, but they also used to have a van deliver supplies every few weeks from some big store somewhere, if I remember rightly. John his self would appear about every fortnight at the post office to collect any post, being as how Marlins was so far off the beaten track and the postie wouldn't go out that far. Pleasant enough bloke, I suppose. He'd smile and say good morning and then he'd get back in his little old Austin car and drive off again, mostly straight back to the house, though sometimes he'd go the other way and stop at the old garage for petrol, not that he could have needed that much, what with him never going anywhere like.'

'He didn't work?' I prompted.

Jacob shrugged. 'Not like we'd call work, young miss,' he replied. 'People said he was some sort of writer, but what he wrote I couldn't tell you, and what he did with his time I couldn't say, not any more than anyone else could, saving perhaps for Minnie Greenway, her being the housekeeper I was telling you about.'

'She'd be dead by now, would she?'

He grinned. 'Less'n she's about a hundred-and-thirty, I reckon she would be. She's dead all right. Died a good twenty years back now and buried in the graveyard at St Cuthbert's over at Melcombe.'

'And John Spigwell, he died before the war, didn't he?'

'Apparently so, not that I ever saw the body, no more than there was a funeral around here, but apparently he was buried up north some place, by whatever family was still left, or so people reckoned at the time.'

'And the family never inherited the house and the land?' Anne-Marie asked.

Jacob shook his head. 'No. There was talk about unpaid death duties, or something, going way back, so I heard. Next thing we knew, they had the military people up there, though what they were up to no one ever found out. Some said it was code breakers, others that they trained people to parachute into France, but it was all just guesswork. Then Jerry flattened the place one night, and that was that. They must have known something we didn't, because they went straight for the place and not a bomb fell anywhere near anything else. Four or five planes, we reckoned, and bloody great explosions you could see and here for miles around. Our lads brought two of them down before they got back to the coast, but the damage was done. A bit after that, they had lorries carting brick rubble away for repair work and then some company bought the rights to whatever woods was left and felled most of it in the space of six months. There was a lot of rebuilding work needed doing at the end of the war, you see.'

'And now it's all farms,' I said. 'Seems a shame they cut down a whole forest like that.'

'Well, man does what man does and people have mouths as needs feeding and heads that needs roofs over them, so things change if they don't stay the way they was,' Jacob said sagely. He peered into the bottom of his empty glass.

Anne-Marie took the hint along with the glass and went back to the bar for a refill.

'What about Meg's Mount?' I steered the subject away from the house. I guessed we had learned as much about it as we were likely to, at least about how it came to its end and the estate was broken up. 'Was that part of the Great Marlins estate?'

'No, all that area ain't owned by no one, as I know of, not unless it's her majesty or the government owns it. No, that's just hills where not a lot happens. They grazed sheep there once, but the grass ain't too good, so they gave it up as a bad job.'

'And do you know who Meg was?'

Jacob raised an eyebrow. 'Well now, I don't say as I'd have known her, but I know who she was supposed to be. It was before even my time, mind, so it's only stories and I can't vouch for the truth in any of it.'

'Go on,' I urged.

He leaned back and looked over at the bar to check on the progress of his new pint. 'Well now, they used to say as how this woman, people called her Mad Meg, used to live somewhere hereabouts. Some said she lived at Marlins, others that she lived somewhere over the far side of the hill, I don't know which is right and I don't suppose it makes much difference.' He paused as if collecting his memories.

'Well, this Mad Meg was supposed to be some sort of

witch, but then they said that about enough old biddies in their time, and I don't believe in that stuff, you understand. But, witch or no witch, the story goes that every new moon, or could be every full moon, she used to strip right off to the buff and go up there and dance all through the night, and then she used to sit on this big rocky outcrop and howl at the sun as it came up.'

'And that's all you know about her?' I couldn't conceal my disappointment.

'That's about all there is to know about her,' Jacob eyed me with interest. 'I was born in eighty-one and she'd have been dead twenty or twenty-five years by then, at least, so by the time I was old enough to listen, well, there'd not have been too many people left about who'd have known the woman personal, like. My old dad did used to say as how he remembered her as a tall, striking creature with dark hair, and that she was not as old as the stories would have had her, but then he'd have only been a young whelp himself when she was still alive, so you can't say anything for certain, can you?'

I couldn't, except that Jacob's father's description would have fitted my Mad Megan to a tee, and running naked around hillsides at new or full moons would have been the sort of crazy thing she might have done. Yet the idea that she thought she might have supernatural powers didn't fit in with what I knew of her.

'So, we don't seem to be much further on, do we?' Andrea remarked as we headed back east along the main road again. 'It probably was your Meg who did the naked rock riding bit, but that doesn't seem to have anything to do with anything, does it?'

At least, I thought as the oncoming headlights picked up the beginning of a drizzling rain, Andrea had cheered up somewhat now that she had been let out of that awful restraining belt. Anne-Marie could be quite horrible to her at times, and although it was all apparently part of their on-going game, I wondered just how much Andrea really appreciated it. 'Well, I don't believe in witchcraft,' I said, 'but then I wouldn't have believed in time travel or body switching, or whatever it is that keeps happening to me, and yet I know now that it's possible.'

'You thinking that maybe Meg started playing around with some sort of dark forces and maybe unwittingly released some sort of power that's working on you?' Anne-Marie suggested. 'I suppose that could be one explanation.'

'It could be,' I agreed, 'but then so could almost any theory. It's not a devil worship thing though, that I'm sure of. There has to be a logical, scientific explanation for it.'

'Except that I doubt anyone could find it,' Andrea said. 'And all we know is that Megan Crowthorne liked to run around naked at night.'

'But it was interesting what the old man said about the death duties stuff dating back for years,' Anne-Marie threw in. 'There's definitely something fishy about the way so many important bits of so many records seem to be missing, like who the estate went to after Meg died, and how she managed to establish a title to it in the first place.'

'And I want to know what happened to Angelina. She's the real key in all this, I'm certain. After all, it's her body I keep popping back into. She needs my help, I'm sure of it.'

'Which you can't give,' Anne-Marie pointed out, 'all the time the mad maidservant and her Viking sidekick keep you all parcelled up in that doggie outfit.' She shuddered. 'That must be really awful, being treated like a dumb animal, and worse.'

'It is,' I assured her. 'I can't do anything for myself and I can't stop anyone else doing anything they like to me, but there has to be some way I can get free of it for long enough to try to sort that Meg bitch out. I'd like to kill her.'

'Except you can't, and you won't, not unless you go back to a time several years later,' Anne-Marie reasoned. 'We know she lived for a good few years after eighteen thirty-nine, so if she's to be stopped, and Angelina is to be freed, it won't be by killing Meg. Besides, as I think you already said, if you do kill anyone back then, it'll be Angelina who has to face the music for it and she'd probably end up on the scaffold.'

'Hey, there's a point,' Andrea said suddenly. 'How about we try checking back through the old records to see if she was ever hanged? That way we'd know if you were supposed to kill Meg or Hacklebury for her and it wouldn't really be your fault. After all, you can't change history, can you? Something to do with the *paradox theory*, or something like that.'

'No,' I said, 'I don't think I'd like to know the answer to that one, not just yet. If Angelina did kill Hacklebury, or if it was me killed him for her, then that'll happen again as it's already happened, if that makes any sense.'

'Then everything else will happen as it's already happened,' Andrea insisted, 'so there's not much point in you being dragged back there over and over again.'

'Unless it's to protect Angelina's sanity,' I suggested, 'to ease some of her suffering and help her get through to whatever conclusion eventually happened. Besides, point or no point, it keeps happening, and I don't have any control over it.'

'And the more you can learn about the people involved,' Anne-Marie added, 'the better your chances of both of you surviving unscathed.'

Chapter Seven

That night I dreamed I went back again and for a moment I thought I had time-hopped, except that when I tried to look down at myself I saw I didn't have a body. I seemed to be a spirit looking down and watching a scene being played out over which I had no control and in which I took no part.

I was in a large room of the house again, but a different room from any I had seen when I was there. The curtains were drawn and the lamps were lit, which suggested it was night. A fire burned in the grate in a tall fireplace but the flames themselves were small, lit more for comfort and effect than for warmth. Several large padded chairs, a sofa and a long chaise lounge, were arranged around the room and on the latter Gregory Hacklebury reclined wearing a dark-red silk robe with matching slippers and smoking a large cigar.

As I watched, the door at the far end of the room opened and Meg entered. Behind her followed the maid girl, Polly, whose hands I saw had been tied together in front of her by what looked like a long length of silk ribbon. She wore her normal uniform except that the long white pinafore was missing and there was no little starched cap on her head. Her eyes looked red and I guessed she had been crying.

'I've brought the wretched girl to you for punishment, sir,' Meg said, turning to push Polly ahead of her. 'Erik caught her trying to take the bitch's head off to feed her some pieces of meat she had stolen from the kitchen.'

'I see,' Hacklebury drawled, staring up at Polly where she now stood before him, her eyes downcast. 'And what have you got to say for yourself, girl?'

'I… I'm truly very sorry, sir,' she murmured, 'but I didn't think it would do no harm seeing as the scraps was going to be thrown out anyway, and that poor girl… well, whatever she's done, I knew she hadn't eaten anything proper for days.'

'And so you took it upon yourself to look after her dietary needs, did you?' Hacklebury enquired pleasantly.

'I just… I just thought she needed a bit of something solid in her, to save her getting poorly, like, sir.'

'You did, did you?' He raised an eyebrow. 'You decided, all by yourself, that my orders and Miss Meg's orders were totally inadequate and so you were going to remove part of the stupid wench's punishment? Tell me, Polly, how would you like to spend a month in such a suit yourself? Mr Pottinger is delivering us several new ones later this week and I'm sure we could accommodate you.'

I saw the girl's face turn ashen. 'Oh no, sir!' she cried, raising her bound wrists in supplication. 'No sir, please, I beg you, not *that!*'

'Then perhaps I should turn you out on the streets again and tell the local magistrate about your little criminal adventures in Bath? How many unfortunate fellows had their purses lifted by your bully-boy associate before I came along? It would be Australia for you, at the very least, or a pretty dance at the end of a rope.'

'Sir, I'm sorry!' Polly wailed. 'It shan't happen again, sir, God's honest truth, as He's my witness!'

So that was it, I thought, that was why Polly seemed to go along with all of Meg's extravagances and didn't try to interfere. Hacklebury had over her that she was a criminal, and the sort of crimes she had been involved in more often than not meant a capital sentence. The fact that Hacklebury couldn't turn her in without risking her spilling his own beans probably hadn't occurred to the silly wench.

'I know it shan't happen again,' Hacklebury said placidly, 'because I am going to teach you a severe lesson in obedience, a lesson you shall not forget for a very long time, my girl. Meg, you may untie her hands now, help her out of her dress and petticoats, and then check to see that her corset is good and tight. If it is, then later you will find her a smaller size and lace her into it once the stripes fade from her backside as a reminder to her.'

Bastard, I thought. As with Angelina, he was turning a supposed fashion accessory into an instrument of torture, an instrument that could be worn undetected by anyone other than the wearer. Going about the daily chores of a maid even in an ordinary corset would have been laborious enough, but to be really tightly laced would be murder.

Polly was quickly stripped of her uniform, which consisted of two long petticoats and an additional shift she wore over her corset, a plain garment with thick laces. Beneath this she had on a pair of voluminous pantaloons that tied about her knees over black cotton stockings, and simple laced shoes with small heels. Meg then immediately checked the corset's lacing and declared it to be far too slack.

'I'll check this myself every morning from now on,' she declared, drawing in on each of the laces in turn. I saw Polly wince, but in truth, the corset fully closed would have been nowhere near as severe as the last one I had worn. Meg also knew this, for she quickly commented on the fact. 'We'll have a much smaller set of stays for you in the morning,' she promised. 'These are for a fat slovenly pig and you wouldn't like people to think you're a fat slovenly pig, would you Polly?'

'No, miss!' the poor girl gasped. 'No, I shouldn't like that!'

'There,' Meg said at last, retying the laces. 'That's as tight as this one gets.' She walked back around in front of Polly and peered down at the girl's pale bosom, which had now been lifted somewhat higher. I saw tiny brown freckles and two thin little blue veins just beneath the surface of her skin. 'She is quite ready for you now, master, unless you wish me to remove her drawers as well?'

'No, that will not be necessary,' Hacklebury said, rising. 'Just put her over the red chair there and tie her wrists to the arms and her ankles to the back legs. It doesn't do to have a girl moving about during punishment.' He turned away and walked to the far wall, where a long sideboard sat beneath a large landscape painting. He opened the cupboard at one end and extracted a selection of canes, which he brought back and laid out on the chaise lounge while Meg set about the task of tying Polly down to the chair.

The maid, her eyes wide and glistening with unshed tears, was made to move behind the heavily padded back of the red armchair and to bend forward over it, laying her arms out along the padded wooden arms whilst Meg, with two lengths of the same material that had been used earlier, tied each of her wrists firmly in turn. Then, from a pocket in her long dress, the older woman drew out two lengths of cord and with these she proceeded to draw Polly's ankles apart and to tie them to the back legs of what was now a very effective whipping horse. The girl's bottom was raised invitingly, unprotected save by the thin material of her pantaloons. Meg then crossed to where Hacklebury was now testing each cane in turn for suppleness and spoke to him quietly, so that the apprehensive prisoner might not hear. I, however, heard every word she said quite clearly.

'I suppose you'll want to fuck the silly bitch afterwards. I can't imagine you being able to say no to such an available target.'

'It'll do her good to know who is master around here,' Hacklebury replied serenely. 'She's a little too flighty about the place, you know, always trying to give me the eye. Probably imagines I might take a fancy to her.'

'She's pretty enough, in a stupid way, but I doubt she ever thought to win your cock whilst bent over a chair with a red raw arse. Yes, you give her a good old-fashioned rogering afterwards. It'll make her think a bit differently then, I reckon. And now, if you have no further need of my services for a while, I think I'll go and see how my little Sheba bitch is getting on. I'd bring her up for you, but I doubt you'll be in the mood for her after you've finished with this little bumpkin.' And with that, she left the room.

Perhaps the worst part of any physical punishment is waiting for it to begin and Hacklebury clearly understood that, for he seemed in no hurry. Instead, he walked slowly around his helpless victim, stroking her back and then her buttocks before reaching down to run his fingers tantalisingly across her bulging cleavage. 'How long is it that you've been with me now, girl?' he asked, gently stroking the nape of her neck with the back of his hand.

Polly sniffed back her tears. 'About two years, I think, sir,' she replied in a shaky voice. 'Quite a time, and I've always tried to be good, sir, honest.'

'Well, I'm going to teach you that you need to try harder, Polly,' he said sternly. 'I'm going to teach you just how hard you need to try and how good you need to be. Otherwise, I'll let Miss Meg have you to play with the same as she's doing with another very disobedient little bitch. Understand?'

'Yes, sir, I understand.'

'Good.' He stepped back and picked up the cane he had finally selected. He flexed it once more and then, positioning himself solidly beside Polly in line with her buttocks, he swung his arm in a wide arc. The whippy instrument cut through the air with a sharp hissing sound and struck the girl's bottom across both cheeks with a high-pitched crack that immediately elicited a shrill scream of agony from her.

'Silence!' Hacklebury roared. 'You must learn to take your punishment quietly or else I shall have you gagged, and leave you gagged for a whole day.' Again the cane swished down and there was another wicked crack upon impact, but this time Polly let out only a stifled groan from between her firmly sealed lips. 'Much better,' he muttered grimly. 'Much better.' Another stroke, followed by another crack, and Polly could not restrain a sob of anguish. I could see that her eyes were screwed shut and that there were fresh tears glistening on her cheeks.

A fourth and fifth stroke were delivered, each one causing the round bottom to jump upon impact and its poor owner to groan and gasp. I doubted she would be able to maintain her self-control for much longer and hoped the punishment would soon be over, for even though the girl had been rough and rude with me as Angelina, I still did not like to see another human being suffer and having been thrashed similarly myself now, I knew how terribly she must be suffering.

Finally came the sixth and, as it turned out, final cut. Polly began to sob openly then, her shoulders heaving as tears streamed down her face. She tried to plead but her words were an incoherent jumble. It was easy to guess, however, that she was promising anything, and everything, to her master in the desperate hope of being spared further punishment.

'That will do for now, Polly,' Hacklebury said severely. 'Stop your stupid snuffling,' he admonished her, 'and listen to what I have to say.'

Sensing that the terrible caning was over, she gradually managed to stifle her sobs and I saw her shoulders relax somewhat she was so relieved.

'Now then, my girl,' her master said when she had calmed down, 'you have been properly punished, not just for your disobedience today but also for your generally impudent attitude. You seem to think you can do almost anything you please around here and I have to tell you that that is not the case. You are my servant and you will do precisely what I tell you to do, or whatever Miss Meg tells you to do on my behalf. You seem to think that being a pretty girl is enough to excuse your lack of discipline and respect,' he went on as he began fumbling with the sash of his robe. 'You need to understand that prettiness is no substitute for respect, for I can find any amount of pretty girls to amuse me. Perhaps I should replace you with one such?'

'No, sir, please,' she begged. 'I'll do anything you want of me, sir, honest I will.'

'I know you will, Polly.' His robe fell open to reveal a rampant erection as he stepped in front of her, seized her by the hair, forcing her head up to confront his excited state. Her eyes grew big and round, but not, I thought, from fright. 'You know what I'm going to do now, don't you, Polly?' he asked quietly.

She mumbled softly, 'Yes, sir.'

'That's right, I'm going to fuck you. I'm going to fuck you just to show you that you are mine to do with as I please, and you will remain mine until I decide to be rid of you.' He released his grip on her hair and allowed her head to fall as he moved around behind her again. He reached down between her legs, and I guessed he was untying the ribbons that held her pantaloons closed at the crotch. Sure enough, after only a momentary delay, he moved in closer to her, grasping his cock in his right hand and guiding its swollen helmet towards its target. I saw Polly's head come up again as she felt the first contact against her entrance, her lips parted in breathless anticipation.

'Yes,' I heard Hacklebury say, 'that's quite nice, isn't it, Polly?' His hips thrust forward and I knew he was entering her as I saw her lips quivering and her fingers clenching and unclenching. 'How does that feel now, Polly?' he demanded calmly, holding a statue-like pose pressed hard against the smooth globes he had just finished treating so mercilessly.

She sighed, 'It feels good, sir!' Then she moaned and I realised that the stupid girl actually meant it. Hacklebury had caned her arse, talked to her like she was dirt, now he was taking her when she was in no position to resist him, and yet she was actually enjoying it.

But then, I thought as he began to thrust in and out of her and her moans grew louder and louder, who was I to criticise her? She was just some poor street waif without the benefit of knowledge or education, whereas I…

I was awake again, lying in the dark with the images from my dream still fresh and clear in my mind. I sat up, swung my legs off the bed and padded across to the window, drawing back the curtain to peer outside. It was still dark and the clock on the bedside table showed it was just after four o'clock in the morning. I let the curtain fall and made my way back to sit on the end of the bed, wondering whether to put the light on and find my cigarettes, or whether to just get back under the covers and try to go back to sleep.

But I did not want to sleep again, not yet, even though I was still tired. The dream had been so real… I knew it had been more than just the product of my subconscious thoughts. I had been back there again, I was certain, though this time not as Angelina but as an unseen observer. The scene I had witnessed had been very revealing as well as traumatic, but I feared it had revealed as much to me about myself as it had about any of the participants.

I fumbled in the darkness until I found a dressing gown I slipped around my shoulders, and then I opened the door leading out onto the upstairs passage. A small nightlight burned over the top of the stairs and I made my way on tiptoe towards it, not wanting to disturb either Anne-Marie or Andrea, for I needed some time on my own to think and evaluate.

Downstairs in the kitchen, I closed the door, put the light on and took the electric kettle to the tap to fill it. A cup of tea and a cigarette were just the thing right now. I had picked up my packet together with my lighter before leaving the bedroom. A smoke would help me to concentrate, I reasoned. I plugged in the kettle, switched it on, and turned to pull a chair out from beneath the table while I waited for the water to boil.

Yes, that dream had definitely been more than just a dream.

I took out a cigarette and lit it, drawing on it deeply.

How had it all worked? Why had I not needed a body to go back this time around? And why had I been taken back to witness that dreadful scene? I had suspected well enough that Hacklebury would be little different with his servants than he had been with me, his supposed wife, but to actually see him doing it, and in such a brutally casual fashion...

The man was a pig, a bully, a sadist, a... words failed me, but the rage within me was building, an anger that was in some ways directed at myself for my own weaknesses. That bastard and his psychotic woman had treated me even worse than they had Polly, and yet had I not surrendered in much the same way, losing myself in the lusts they had somehow managed to stir in me? And had I not then surrendered in a similar manner, albeit under different circumstances, to Anne-Marie and her temptations and machinations?

What the hell was I doing, both here in the present and back there nearly a century-and-a-half ago? Had I no pride, no discipline, no sense of right and wrong? But of course I did, I reasoned as I stood up again to find a clean mug. Of course I had all of those things, but I also had little choice in the matter, at least in the past, where it wasn't *my* body that betrayed me. But this was my body here and now, and this was the body that had succumbed to the lures Anne-Marie had spun for it, allowing itself to be used as little more than a toy, allowing itself to be publicly exhibited, allowing itself the luxury of every sensation that stirred within it.

I made tea, finished my first cigarette and promptly lit another. Outside it was still dark and would be for another three-and-a-half hours, at least. Three-and-a-half hours until dawn and my two new friends sound asleep upstairs. Time enough for me to creep back up to my room, dress, and then slip away, not to Rose Lea but back to my own home, back to safety and sanity, normality and love. But also, sooner or later, back to Megan Crowthorne and Gregory Hacklebury, back in time yet again to mingle my fate with Angelina's, to wrestle with her destiny as I was now wrestling with my own conscience, back over and over again until it was settled, one way or the other. No, running away was no solution because the fault and the danger lay not here but somewhere inside myself, with something that had risen from the depths of time, and from depths of depravity I now suspected must lie hidden within each and every one of us waiting only for the right summons, the right trigger, to surface in all its black ugliness.

I had switched the kettle on again to brew a second cup of tea when Andrea appeared in the kitchen, or I should say Andy, for the wig and make-up were both gone and he was dressed in a baggy pair of pale blue pyjamas.

'Bit of a shock?' he asked, smiling at the look on my face. He moved past me and reached up to take another mug down from a row of hooks. 'I thought I heard someone come down earlier,' he said, dropping tea bags into both our mugs. 'Couldn't sleep?'

I hesitated for an instant but then related the dream to him, though I didn't mention any of my personal misgivings and the reason I had not wanted to risk going back to sleep straightaway.

'Spooky, huh?' He poured the now boiling water and reached for the sugar. 'And you're sure it wasn't just images surfacing from inside you?'

'Well, they probably did surface from inside me, but something must have put them there in the first place. No, that scene took place, all right. I don't know how, or why, but I'm as sure of that as I've ever been of anything in my life.'

'Well, as I said before, that doesn't help us much. We could have worked out for ourselves that Hacklebury enjoyed beating his maids and shagging them and we know that mad Meg tended to pander to his little foibles.'

'Yes, but I'd assumed it was because she wanted to keep him under control for herself,' I said. 'I assumed she was in love with him but now I don't think she was. Yes she was mad and yes she was cruel, but she didn't love him. She wanted to have control over him, but not for himself. No, it was all about money, land and power.'

'Well, if that record we saw was correct, then she got

the land, all right,' Andy reminded me. We took our mugs and moved back over to the table. 'The only thing is,' he added, 'we don't know how she managed it, or whether she managed to keep it for long after she got it.'

'I'm not sure any of that stuff really matters, Andy. We've been chasing around trying to discover the results without tackling the causes. Meg was the cause of all the trouble, but Angelina is the mysterious cause of me going back into her body. I don't really have any real sense of her when I'm there, but I reckon she wasn't what we'd call a hard case, not in any way, shape or form. She resisted Hacklebury initially, we know, or at least I do from what was said and from those odd little flashes I was getting, but I don't think she was up to taking the physical stuff for long and somehow she sort of blanked out, at which point I was whipped in as a substitute. That's as near as I can work it out.'

'And until you get her out of her fix, you reckon you'll keep getting pulled back there?' Andy asked soberly.

I nodded. 'Yes, I think so. She needs help and somehow she's managed to reach out to me across one hundred-and-thirty odd years, though I doubt whether she knows she's doing it, let alone how. Maybe when the pain got so severe it triggered some power deep inside her, something that's in all of us but that we never usually know about, let alone get to use.'

'Well, pain can trigger all sorts of things, can't it?' he replied darkly, avoiding my eyes. 'I think we both know that, don't we?'

'Yes, but I'd rather not talk about that, if you don't mind. I'm not feeling very proud of myself right now, if you must know.'

'Nor am I.' He reached across the table and laid his hand over mine. 'I'm just a stupid little idiot who plays even more stupid games and who likes dressing up and pretending to be something he isn't. It's hiding from reality, I know, but I enjoy it and I can't stop myself. I wish I could.'

'You do?' I smiled across at him. 'But you do make a very pretty girl, you know.'

'Yes, I know,' he muttered. 'But I'd probably do it even if I didn't. I'd just look that bit more stupid, that's all.'

'But Anne-Marie encourages you, doesn't she?'

'Yes, but that's Anne-Marie for you. Don't get me wrong, I love her dearly, but she knows how to manipulate and control people and she likes getting her own way. You shouldn't blame yourself for anything that's happened lately. She knows just which buttons to push when she wants something.'

'You mean she wanted… wants me?'

'At the moment, yes, you're a sort of challenge to her, an opportunity for her to prove just how clever she can be. She sensed something when she met you, she worked on it, and you fell right into it.'

'Am I that obvious, then?'

'No, no more than any of us,' Andy said consolingly. 'We've all got our weaknesses and you'd be surprised how similar they often are. I've learned *that* even if I've learned little enough else. You mentioned pain and pain is only a pinprick away from passion. All the dressing up and tying up stuff is just an additional cover to hide behind, a way of burying what we think is our real selves and letting out the gremlins.'

'But why would Anne-Marie want to let my gremlins

out in the first place?' I demanded.

He smiled. 'Because they're there, and because she knows how to, it's as simple as that. It's a challenge and a control thing. But I think the time is coming for me to take a bit more control for myself and to try and explain to her that I need to be my own person a bit more, even if that person does wear a skirt and stockings some of the time. But it might not be easy; I don't want to hurt her. Like I said, I love her but I'm not *in* love with her, not like I am with you.'

'With me?' I gasped and nearly dropped the mug that was halfway to my lips. 'You're in love with *me*? Are you kidding?'

'Cross my heart and hope to die,' he said, gesturing with his free hand over his chest. 'I fell in love with you the first time I saw you, except I couldn't say or do anything because Anne-Marie had discovered you, as it were, and as usual good little Andrea was supposed to just go with the flow.'

'I never realised... I didn't have the slightest idea,' I said, genuinely amazed by this sudden revelation.

'And now you're going to tell me I'm stupid because you obviously can't feel the same way about me, and that sort of thing.'

'I... I don't know,' I replied honestly. 'I mean, I never even thought about it. This whole thing so far has just been, well, you know what I mean.'

'Playing games, yes, I know what you mean, but it got sort of serious for me and when we... well, you know, when we did it those times, there was more to it than just the lust thing. It was actually harder for me to do that with you than it would have been if you'd been someone else. Oh, I'm not explaining this very well at all!'

Now it was my turn to rest a consoling hand over his. 'I think you're explaining it very well,' I said truthfully. 'Yes, I do understand, and yes, I can understand why you felt you couldn't say anything and just how difficult it would be where Anne-Marie is concerned. You think she might be jealous?'

'Yes, but not jealous in the usual sort of way, she just wants it to be her doing if the two of us end up as an item.' He smiled again thinly. 'We're supposed to be the followers, you see, and if Annie doesn't think of it first, then it can't possibly be a good idea.'

'Well, it might not be a good idea to say anything to her just yet. I mean, there's no telling what might happen in the future. And while I'm not saying no, well, I sort of only just met you. I mean, I know a bit about Andrea, the randy little bitch with a cock in her knickers, but I've hardly met the boy behind her. Let's give it a bit of time, shall we?'

'Yes, you're right,' Andy sighed. 'Besides, I don't expect you'll find much about me that you fancy hanging onto for any great length of time.'

'Oh, I don't know about that. I can think of one thing, at least.' I smiled. 'Look,' I said evenly, 'it's still only five o'clock and it won't be light for ages yet. Sitting around on these hard chairs is giving me a numb bum and it's warmer up in the bedrooms.'

'You mean...?'

'I mean come upstairs to bed with me as Andy for a change. And yes, I do mean to fuck, or make love, or whatever you prefer to call it.'

It was a curious sensation sliding under the covers with someone whom I'd had sex with several times before, including in public, and then snuggling up to one another like a couple of novice virgins, neither of us sure who should make the first move or what that first move ought to be. In the end, after a few minutes of silence, I decided I should take the initiative.

I raised my head, leaned across him and lowered my mouth to his, pressing gently against it before slowly sliding my tongue between his lips. His arms came carefully around me, holding me, the warmth of his body permeating my thin nightgown, the slight tremor in his muscles seemingly amplified as his chest pressed against my breasts.

'That's nice,' I whispered as I drew back slightly. 'This whole thing is very nice.' I reached down and felt for his groin, massaging gently when I found his cock already half aroused. He sighed and I felt his fingers exploring my right breast searching for my nipple. 'Mm,' I said, 'yes, that's so very sensitive there…'

'God, Teenie, I do want you so!' he whispered. 'I want you more than anything, but I don't want to ruin anything.'

'You won't,' I assured him. 'You won't ruin anything at all. Just relax and let me show you.' It reminded me of how I had all but raped Andrea before, with her flat on her back and her stiff cock unable to resist my advances, but this was different, for now we both had a choice and that choice was shared.

I rolled over and up on top of Andy, straddling him, and then lifted my weight off him to draw down his pyjama bottoms as far as his knees. The room was still in complete darkness so I worked by touch, running my fingers back up the front of his thighs and closing them around his now full erection. 'Whose is this?' I whispered.

'Yours,' he replied softly. 'All yours.'

'Yes,' I said, 'it's all mine.' And I took it, possessed it, devoured it, sliding myself down its entire length to settle myself on him, squirming my hips and flexing my internal muscles to grip him tightly. I felt his hands running up my stomach beneath my nightgown, his warm fingers stroking my flesh and then reaching up further to cup my breasts. His thumbs flicked across my nipples, which were now as hard as brass buttons, and so sensitive that his touch brought a cry from the back of my throat. 'Yes,' I breathed, 'all mine, Andy. You're all mine now!'

Whether or not I was ready to be all his, I neither knew nor cared at that moment, for it was a decision that would probably be made for me, for better or for worse, and only in the fullness of time...

Dawn. A deserted country road, deserted except for a small, dark-haired figure walking through the early mist and occasionally casting glances back over her shoulder as if fearful of what may be behind her. Because despite the bright uniform jacket hanging loosely about her shoulders, she is most definitely female. Her black tresses fall to her waist and her full, brown-skinned breasts are visible as the coat flaps open and closed in the breeze. Beneath the jacket she is naked, her bare feet now almost white from the dried mud and dust over which she has been trekking. She has travelled many miles now by night, the darkness her only protection as she moves determinedly towards her goal.

As the first red-gold tip of the sun glints between two

dark-green hills in the east, she pauses to look away from the road over trees and fields, casting about for the sanctuary she needs while the new day takes its course again towards nightfall. Her eyes narrow as they fall upon a white smudge in the distance and she continues on her way again, still following the road. She knows she has a little time yet in which to settle herself as the smudge becomes larger, revealing darker outlines that form themselves into the identifiable rectangles of windows and doors.

She turns off the road onto a narrower track that is even more rutted and uneven but that takes her in a direct line towards the house. She climbs up a short slope to a small stand of sapling trees where she stops to observe the building from a hidden vantage point, noting the outhouses behind it and in particular the low shape of the hencoop.

As she stands there, the door of the house opens and a figure appears, another female, older than our traveller by a good many years and much more suitably attired against the chill dawn air. She carries a heavy basket which she sets down beneath the hemp line stretching between two rough-hewn poles, and takes from it the first item of her freshly laundered burden, tossing it over the line and securing it there with wooden pegs.

Indira smiles to herself and squats down on her haunches, her back resting against one of the trees. The farmer's wife continues to peg out her washing – blankets, sheets, breeches, a skirt and two dresses, dark stockings of rough wool – and the sun continues to climb in the sky. The rural day has begun and already the farmer is up and about and ready for his daily grind. He emerges from the house behind the woman and turns away to the nearest field and the two heavy horses Indira has observed grazing there.

It is the beginning of harvest time and the ripened crops must be gathered while the weather holds. The farmer – or is it his son? – will be busier even than usual, and so will his wife and any other family member big enough to wield a sickle or fill and carry a basket. The house will be empty and the hencoop will be as full as the washing line.

Indira smiles and settles down more comfortably to wait. The rumbling in her stomach will soon be answered and the rough coat, which has been her only protection against the elements for the past three days, will soon be discarded. She will leave the few coins which are in its pocket, leave them on the table in the kitchen of the farmhouse. It will be enough to pay for the hen she will take and for the few clothes she will need to better attire herself for the remainder of her journey.

She hopes it will be more than enough, for she is not a thief. They have taken her honour from her, it is true, but she knows she can remain honourable in herself, regardless. She will pay for her wants and needs, and pay for them with money that is the very least she is due after what the leering, jeering soldiers have taken from her.

She closes her eyes and relaxes. Sleep, if only for an hour or two, is much needed and she will awake with fresh determination to continue.

'I shall come, my little love,' she whispers to the gentle breeze. 'I shall come to you soon, have no fear.'

Chapter Eight

I opened my eyes and saw that darkness had given way to full daylight. Bright early morning sunlight streamed in through the narrow window vents at the top of the walls comprising my kennel prison cell. My legs and arms were once again stiff and all but useless, and this time I resolved not to struggle to get myself upright. Erik would arrive soon and lift me over and up without the need for any undignified and exhausting struggles on my part.

I cursed silently. I had been snatched back again and this time from a moment that was proving to be very special for me as well as for Andy. Hopefully, I would eventually be returned to it. But what further miseries would I have to endure here first, and would Andy realise what was happening back in my own time?

The minutes ticked away and it was beginning to look as though Erik was going to be unusually late for work this morning. Always until now he had arrived early, within minutes of my waking, or so it seemed. Had something happened since I had last been here? Had perhaps several days, or even weeks, passed? I had no way of telling. All I could do was wait.

At last I heard the sound of his heavy boots outside and a moment later he entered my cell, ducking under the door lintel and dropping a sack into the corner. He stood for a moment looking down at me before he gathered me up effortlessly, lifting me into the air and turning me over to deposit me back in my required all-fours position. Then, to my surprise, he began removing the dogface mask, and prised my mouth open to release the clamps that held my tongue plate in position.

'Thank you,' I said, meaning it. I looked up into his placid face. 'Or do I still have to say woof?' I asked sarcastically.

'Woof you do not say the moment for at least,' he told me. 'But talk loudly must you not, for Miss Meg angry would be if she knew permitted to talk at all you were.'

'Miss Meg can go fuck herself!' I said testily. 'She's a nasty, vicious bitch who could probably do with a good fucking herself to get her stupid head right!' It was a ridiculous insult and very childish but it seemed to amuse Erik no end.

'Fucking of Miss Meg indeed a fine thought might be,' he chuckled. 'Icebergs I have seen that warmer are.'

'And a lot less dangerous, unless you happened to be on the Titanic. Oh, sorry,' I apologised, 'that hasn't happened yet.'

'Pardon please, but titanic very large means, does it not?'

'Yes, it does, but it was… um, it will be, the name of a ship.'

'A big ship?' he asked almost eagerly. 'With big sails?'

'A big ship, yes, but big sails, no.'

'Then big oars, in the olden times like as with my ancestors it was?' He made rowing motions with his arms.

I shook my head. 'No, not oars, but a big engine driven by steam.'

'Ah!' he nodded. 'The trains they have engines with steam. Seeing one I have been… no, two. Very noisy, very dirty, and very dangerous, I think, for too fast are they going.'

'They'll get faster, believe me, and even more dangerous.'

'Food have I brought for you,' he announced, indicating the sack. 'Meat and bread and fresh milk.'

'Thank you,' I said, and looked down my body past my padded bosom at my flattened stomach. 'I don't suppose...?' I began, but then shook my head. 'No, Miss Meg certainly wouldn't approve of you loosening my laces, and if you did and I pigged out you'd probably not be able to get them closed again. Oh, well.'

'Stand up you may and feed you I shall,' Erik said.

With great relief, I straightened up and let my elongated arms hang relaxed at my sides.

'Slowly you must chew, though, for cramps else you will surely get.'

I nodded and waited whilst he opened the sack and began spreading its contents out on the floor. 'Tell me something, Erik,' I said quietly. 'Just how much do they pay you to do this job?'

He turned and looked up at me from his crouched position. 'Money I get that is very good, more than getting I was when fishing.'

'Ah, you were a fisherman, were you? On a boat at sea?'

He nodded.

'And then you came here to England?'

'First went I to Prussia, fighting in their army to be, but then of fighting there was none to be done, so then to France and then to here, to Manchester, big city with many people. I work on canals. Very strong, see?' He flexed his bicep to illustrate a point that didn't need proving.

'And then you met Hacklebury, the master?'

'No, first I meet Miss Meg when very sick in the stomach I was. She give me medicine that stomach is made better by, and then a job she offers me travelling with her to guard her body. She bring me back to here and guard her body I still do, but also now I guard your body.'

'Do you guard her body the same way you guard mine?' I asked mischievously. 'You know, fucky-fuck stuff, and all that?'

He looked genuinely astonished. 'Not indeed!' he said in a tone that suggested the Pope was more likely to be a whoremonger than he was to even dream of such a thing.

'Ah, I see. That's Hacklebury's department, is it?'

Erik looked bewildered.

I rephrased the question. 'Sir Gregory and Miss Meg, they do the fucky thing, do they?'

'Knowing that I am not, but thinking it I do not either,' he replied. 'Miss Meg… no, she does not, I think, not even with the master.'

That, I thought, was quite interesting and seemed to bear out my most recent theory concerning the unlikely couple. Meg wanted control of Gregory, of course, but she wasn't trying to get it by offering him her own body, and neither did she love him, so it was all a mercenary thing where she was concerned. But what leverage did she have if not the oldest one of all?

I chewed and ate the meat slowly, sucked two or three pieces of bread and drank the milk, which was still warm from the cow and foreign to my modern taste buds. I did not particularly like any of it, but I needed to keep my strength up as much as possible for it could yet be a long time before I had even the slightest opportunity to escape, and I didn't want to find myself fainting away if the chance presented itself.

All too soon, it was time for the gag and the mask again. Erik had the good grace to look apologetic and he promised he would take the things off me again as soon as he could, but for now I was to be walked in the woods and then paraded on the lawn before the library windows, probably, I assumed, so that Gregory Hacklebury could be reminded of the control Meg now had over his wife, the bitch dog she had created.

To my relief, when we arrived at the back of the house there was no sign of either Hacklebury or Meg, though two maids did appear from the direction of the kitchen. They stood watching and giggling as I was paraded back and forth across the lawn, though admittedly at some distance from us. I peered out at them from my mask, trying to see if I could recognise one of them as Polly, but although the taller girl looked vaguely familiar, neither one of them was the poor maid from my dream. Not that it would have made much difference, I reflected as Erik turned me to walk back down through the trees, but at least it gave me something to think about for a few minutes rather than just plodding mindlessly along at the end of my lead.

A dog's life, I concluded grimly, could be a very boring life indeed.

Which abruptly gave me cause to wonder just why I had been transported back this time, for my previous visits had apparently been timed to coincide with particularly traumatic stages in Angelina's captivity. Oh, this dog thing was traumatic enough and I fully expected Erik to take advantage of my helplessness yet again before the day was much older, but it did not compare with the earlier thrashings, nor even with the shock I had experienced upon being transformed into a mock canine for the first time.

Unless...

Maybe I was now supposed to inhabit this body fulltime, keeping Angelina safely out of the firing line, so to speak. After all, my breaks back in my own time did not appear to bear any direct relationship to the passage of time here. If I were now being returned to this body at the same time and place as when I left it previously, that would certainly protect Angelina's sanity. Yes, it made sense. If there had been any continuity gaps, they could only have been during hours when this body had been sleeping, when it would have made no difference which of us was in occupation.

Lucky little Angelina, I mused as we once again came in sight of my kennel and yard. Not only saved the pain and the shock, but the boredom, too. And yet, although everything seemed to have settled into a mundane routine, I could not get away from the feeling that something felt slightly different and that something, possibly something of great importance, was about to happen.

There are many forms of torture in this world. Some are physical and involve the inflicting of pain. Some are psychological and can range from humiliating the victim to imposing a regiment of deprivation not only of the senses but also of more abstract things like freedom.

Take, for example, boredom. Boredom, combined with

humiliation and the sense of being forgotten and neglected, is a very effective form of torture, indeed. I stood in the middle of my tiny world, the sunlight filtering in through the vents in the wall, and through the door beyond the short passageway outside my cell, my only contact with the outside world until Erik chose to return again.

He had indeed chosen to use me after our outing but he had done so with a detached attitude, entering me and pumping in and out of my defenceless sex as if it were a routine chore and not an act to be savoured. Afterwards he patted my head, gave me water through the funnel and left me without another word. For who needs to exchange words when all the words that can be said have been said? Besides, I would still be here when he returned and still be as available to him, a four-legged parody useful only for base relief and the amusement of captors who now seemed to be tiring of me. It seemed I was surplus to any real requirements, my presence a burden even though my continued existence was presumably still preferable to my death, at least for the moment. Whatever plans Meg and Hacklebury had were being pursued without the requirement of my immediate involvement. If they needed to keep me alive, they were doing so in the cruellest of ways, yet even this unbearable situation might prove to be only temporary.

Even if they did break me and temper my will to theirs, my usefulness to them was surely limited. Once they got whatever it was they wanted, I would become a liability and a potentially dangerous one, at that. Far easier to slit my throat, choke the life out me with a length of cord or slip something into my food than to keep me around; simple, quick and fatal. No more Angelina and maybe no more Teena, either. I pondered the threat to my existence and waited. There was nothing else I could do but wait, a sorry four-legged captive with no voice and no face save for the pug-like leather visage they had given me. *It shouldn't happen to a dog*, I thought grimly, and then might have laughed had I been able to, for it *wasn't* happening to a dog. It was happening to me.

The sun continued to move across the sky, its steady progress revealed only by the shifting shadows. Somewhere outside birds twittered and called to each other and somewhere, in another world, in another time, another body waited in another limbo, a body to which I fervently prayed I would soon be returning.

Not long after darkness fell, the limbo in my little prison came to an end in a way I could never have foreseen. Eric had dropped in earlier for a few minutes, just long enough to unmask me so I could eat, though I had to suffer the gross indecency of feeding myself from a metal bowl on the floor with only my teeth and lips to grab up the morsels. Another bowl was also filled with water and I was thus able to drink at will, at least all the time the leather dog mask remained hanging on the hook by the door. With my tongue still hampered by the clamp, it was no easy or tidy matter to suck in my sustenance, but it was better than starving to death and dehydrating, so when he left me alone, I gratefully took advantage of small mercies.

The problem was that without the need for regular visits to water me Eric would be appearing less, and less. Even if his visits more often than not resulted in us playing doggies together, that was better than being increasingly bored by my confinement. Therefore, when I heard his heavy tread again and saw the flickering lamplight beyond my door, I was actually intensely pleased.

He hung the lantern on the wall, put down the small bag he had been carrying in his other hand and instructed me to stand upright. I had actually already been standing when I heard him approaching but had obediently resumed my dog stance before he arrived. I got back on my feet and stood motionless while he prised my mouth open and loosened the gag clamp to pull it off.

'Thank you,' I said once he had withdrawn the device. I ran my tongue around my mouth, if only to prove to myself that I could still do it. 'I've managed to eat everything,' I said, looking pointedly down at the empty food bowl.

'Good, and now washing you we shall be for smelling bad you are.'

I flushed at this directness but there was no arguing the truth of his statement. Besides, washing meant I would be free of the confining dog suit, if only for a brief interlude. I stood passively while he began tugging at the laces. Then there was the sound of more footsteps outside and he paused as both of us automatically turned our heads in the direction of the door. At this time of night, the only likely visitor was Meg.

Sure enough, she appeared in the doorway, but instead of tossing the expected sneering comment in my direction she remained silent, her face taut and pale, and a moment later I saw the reason for her expression. As she stepped into the room she was followed by a second figure, a shorter, brown- skinned girl with jet-black hair dressed in rough country clothes. She was undoubtedly of Indian origin and had huge, almond-shaped eyes I could tell were the deepest brown even in the dim light.

Immediately I realised that I knew her, or that Angelina knew her, and I knew, too, that her name was Indira, though beyond that there were only confused images and an intense sadness associated with her. However, whatever her relationship with Angelina, it was immediately obvious that Indira was not on Meg's side for in her right hand she held an enormous pistol, the muzzle of which was pressed firmly into the small of Meg's back. In her left hand she gripped the handle of a knife, the blade of which was stained darkly with what could only be blood. She looked straight at Eric, who had frozen in surprised indecision.

'One wrong move from you, you great blond lump, and I'm going to put a hole through this bitch you could fit your head in. Understand?'

Eric gaped at her, but nodded.

I, in the meantime, was stunned to hear such a blunt threat uttered so fiercely by an Indian girl this far back in time in an accent that was clearly not ethnic or even contemporary. Something was very wrong. Or very right…

Indira looked at me, and winked. 'Listen,' she said abruptly, 'I don't really know quite how this has all happened, but it's happened and we have to take advantage of it. First, you need to get out of that lot and put something else on. This bitch is a bit bigger than you, but her dress will have to do until we can find you something better.'

'I… I don't understand,' I gasped. 'Who are you? I mean, I know your name, I think, but where have you come from?'

'Well, if you know my name here then you know more than I do,' the girl replied, and smiled suddenly. 'But yes, you do know my name, and I know yours, Teenie.'

'Andy?' I felt like as though the ground abruptly shifted beneath my feet. 'How? I mean—'

'Haven't got a fucking clue,' my transvestite lover replied, shrugging. 'All I know is that one minute we were quite happily doing the thing we both like doing most and then suddenly I was here, or to be more precise, I was about half a mile or so away, standing just inside a fence where there was a small gap between the palings, next to some guy lying in a heap on the ground with this knife sticking out of the back of his neck. That's where I got this gun. It's a lovely piece of workmanship. Probably not very accurate, but fires a whopping great lead ball.'

'I should have slit your miserable little throat!' Meg hissed. 'You dirty little black whore! You'll pay dearly for this!'

'Whore I may be,' Andy retorted, 'but from what I can see I'm brown, not black, and I happen to be the one holding the big gun and the nasty knife, so shut your mouth if you don't want me to stick this thing in your arse a few times. It looks very sharp to me and would go straight through your skirts as easy as through butter. And *you*,' he pointed the knife at Eric, 'get that stuff off my friend and don't try anything clever unless you want bits of this bitch all over your nice clean shirt. And don't think I won't do it.'

'You only have the one shot, little Indira,' Meg said abruptly. 'Just one shot, and the noise is sure to bring others running. You won't get away.'

'Well, in that case we won't be any worse off than we

already are, will we?' Andy said brightly. 'But *you'll* be very, very dead, which has to be an improvement judging from what my friend has told me about you, Megan Crowthorne. Now shut your noise and get out of your skirt and shoes and don't try anything stupid.'

It took several minutes for Eric to complete the laborious unlacing process, by which time Meg had been standing in her stockings and corset for quite a while. Her eyes were cold with rage but she knew she was impotent in the face of the pistol and, mad or not, she wasn't stupid enough to defy certain death. I dragged her dress over my head and turned so that Eric could fasten the hooks at the back. It was a loose fit, but better than nothing, and certainly an improvement on what I had been wearing.

'The shoes are a waste of time,' I declared, quickly trying one on. 'She must be three sizes bigger than me. I'll be better off barefoot, unless there's something suitable in the next room. There's certainly stuff there we can use to tie these two up with.'

'That's good,' Andy said. It was almost his own voice, or at least a version of Andrea's he used, but not quite, and I was still somewhat in shock at hearing his words emerging from that pretty mouth in that undeniably feminine and alien face. We moved into the next stall, where several items of bondage equipment, along with boots and corsets, were stored.

'Use those,' Andy instructed Erik, pointing to where a pair of thick leather cuffs dangled on a short chain from one of the nails in the wall. 'Buckle them good and tight, with her hands behind her back, and make sure those little lock things are done up properly.

Erik obeyed with alacrity, and though for a moment I

thought Meg was going to resist, she submitted in the end.

'Now you, big boy,' Andy said, waving the pistol at Eric. 'Stand facing the wall and put your hands behind your back and don't forget, one wrong move and the bitch gets it.'

I gaped at Andy, not quite able to take everything in yet and not quite able to believe the silly bugger actually seemed to be enjoying all this. It was a bit like a scene from a James Cagney movie, but neither Meg nor Eric would have been able to appreciate that as Mr Cagney wasn't even a twinkle in his father's eye yet. Come to think of it, his father probably wasn't even a twinkle in his father's eye yet, either.

'Use those metal cuff things, Teenie.' Andy pointed to where a set of steel manacles dangled next to a rather complex arrangement of leather straps. 'They look solid enough to hold even him. My, but you weren't exaggerating, were you? He's a big bugger, for sure!'

Big bugger or not, Eric soon stood as helpless as his mistress and at last I felt we could relax, if only for a little while. 'I still don't understand how you came back here,' I said.

Andy shrugged. 'Who cares? We can think about all that later, but for the moment we need to get as far away from here as possible.'

'And then what?' I demanded. 'I've got no money, I'm wearing a dress that's too big for me and I don't have any shoes. We're miles away from anywhere and we have no way of knowing which way we should go. And if we do manage to get somewhere, what then? I'm supposed to be married to Hacklebury and you've just killed one of his servants, unless it was the man himself.'

'No, you said Hacklebury was dark and the bloke I got the pistol off had fair ginger-coloured hair as far as I could see in the moonlight. But hey, I never killed him. He was already dead when I slipped into this body.'

'Oh, right, so that's okay, then. We just go to court here and tell them how you've come back over a hundred years and weren't in charge of Indira's body when she stabbed the guy. Yes, they'll let us off no problem, and maybe even give us a few guineas for our trouble. You idiot, Andy! All the time you're here in that body, you're Indira and you're responsible in everyone's eyes for anything and everything she's ever done or likely to do, same as she'll be responsible for anything you do while you're in her body.'

I could see Meg's eyes widening as I talked. Whether she fully understood what it was I was saying, and whether or not she believed a word of it, I neither knew nor cared, but I could see that she was both alarmed and baffled. Erik, on the other hand, remained as impassive and expressionless as ever.

I turned to Meg. 'Don't even try to understand,' I said, 'but listen to this and listen very hard, whether it makes sense to you or not. I'm not actually Angelina, but I'm not some double like the one you used for your little wedding farce, either. Don't even try working it out. Let's just say that now the boot is on the other foot and I'm not the sweet little innocent victim you thought you had. After what you've done to me, I feel like taking that knife and cutting your fucking tits off, you bitch, so don't give me even the slightest excuse or I'll make you wish you hadn't been born.' I stopped to catch my breath and turned back to Andy. 'We need clothes, shoes, food and some money,' I said firmly, 'and there's only one place hereabouts where we can get them, and that's up at the house.'

'Where Hacklebury is sure to be, along with those other maids and probably a footman or two,' he pointed out, 'not to mention the charming friends you told us all about.'

'I hadn't overlooked that, but it's dark out and there aren't any lights in the grounds.'

'No electricity here yet,' Andy agreed, 'but they'll have lanterns and candles inside the house.'

'In the main rooms they have plenty of light, but not that much in the rest of the house, especially not in most of the passageways. If I can get inside without being seen, I can probably persuade one of the maids to help us, especially if you give me that knife and I explain how my friend is down here holding a pistol on their dear mistress. Polly and the other girls are just simple souls and they'll frighten easily enough.'

'It all sounds a bit risky to me.' Andy shook his pretty head with its long dark tresses.

'Not if I wait a couple more hours, or so,' I said. 'Unless dear Gregory is planning another house party, they'll all be starting to hit the sack before long. No telly or radio here, don't forget, and they get up early in the morning.'

'But what if anyone comes down here in the meantime? What if these two are missed and they come looking for them?'

'Then we'll have ourselves some more prisoners,' I replied bluntly. 'Besides, Meg here comes and goes all over the place and Erik does what she tells him to like the good boy he is, so if she isn't in the house, Hacklebury will assume she's down here tormenting me for her amusement. He seems to have mostly lost interest in me himself and I don't think he ever actively goes seeking Meg's company. I don't think he likes the bitch.'

'Well, that's one thing we have in common with him,' Andy said, and chuckled. 'But I still don't like it,' he added soberly.

'Neither do I, but we don't have much choice. Neither of us has anything on our feet; we look like a pair of tramps. We won't get five miles like this. And apart from food and clothing, there's probably a coach and horses somewhere around here.' I turned back to Meg. 'Where are the stables, bitch?'

She regarded me with a look that was pure venom, but there was no fear in her eyes now. 'Find them yourself, slut,' she snapped. 'You seem to think you know everything.'

'I know one thing,' I said, brandishing my finger under her nose. 'We're getting out of here with or without any help from you, and if we have to leave you with your throat slit, then that's the way it'll have to be.'

'But Teenie, we already know that...' Andy began.

I glared a warning at him. 'Yes, we do,' I agreed slowly, for I had not forgotten that Megan Crowthorne had still been alive some years after the time we were in now. 'We know a lot, but not everyone has our advantages, *do* they?'

'No, of course not... okay, so we slit the bitch's throat before we go.'

'Maybe,' I said, watching again for some sign of a reaction from Meg. 'We'll have to see. But I don't think we need any help from her, anyway. Erik here will tell us all we need to know, won't you Erik, otherwise I shall cut a line right across Megan's cheeks, and then I'll start

211

carving pretty pictures in her tits.'

It was a threat I could never have carried out, but Erik was not to know that and he quickly gave me directions for the stables, which were apparently only just behind the house. By this time of night, he further assured me, there would be no groom on duty, but I quickly realised that hitching up a team of horses to Hacklebury's carriage would be no job for an amateur.

'Then you'll come with us,' I said simply. 'You and me will get the carriage organised while Indira stays with Meg somewhere close enough to see and hear what's going on. If anything happens to me, she shoots the bitch.'

Erik nodded. 'Understanding I am,' he said sombrely. 'Doing as you wish will I be and of trickery there will be none.'

'Good,' I said. 'I'm glad we understand each other, now we just have to wait a while.' I smiled. 'What shall we do to help pass the time, I wonder?'

Perhaps I was descending to their level, but I didn't really care. Besides, the chance to get back at Meg was far too good to miss.

'Let's get her over that trestle thing, Andy,' I said, pointing to the timber stand over which I had been both whipped and fucked. 'There's plenty of cord.' I thrust Meg towards the trestle and I'm sure she would have resisted had she realised what I intended. However, by the time the light dawned in her cesspit of a brain, it was too late. She had been bent over the trestle and secured to it with her legs spread wide.

I reached down between her thighs and tugged at the ribbon tie at the crotch of her drawers. 'She's as dry as a bone,' I commented, exploring further with my fingers.

'So, Erik my dear, I think maybe you'll need to use that tongue of yours first. Come on, you great ox, get round here on your knees or I'll start cutting her face,' I lied enthusiastically.

It was obvious Erik was more than a little reluctant to obey me, probably because he was in awe of Meg and wondering what she might do to him once she was free again, but for the moment there was nothing he could do save follow my instructions in the hope that doing so would spare his mistress any real harm. He knelt behind her, shuffled forward on his knees, and soon had his head buried between her thighs with his tongue working industriously. The expression on Meg's face almost made my own earlier privations worth the while, for her features contorted with a mixture of rage and disgust, and then slackened into an expression of sheer horror and disbelief as she realised her own body was only marginally less treacherous than Angelina's when faced with certain inescapable stimulus. Very soon she began panting and groaning, wriggling her hips in an effort to escape Erik's tongue and lips, but the bindings held her as immovably as they had once held me, and eventually she realised that resistance was in vain.

'Let's see if we can help,' I murmured, and knelt beside Erik to untie the front of his breeches. To my surprise, I found he was already almost hard, so that a few gentle strokes from my fingers quickly completed the required task. 'Now,' I said, my heart beating madly against my ribcage, 'I think you can fuck her for us, Erik. Yes, stand up and I'll guide you in and she can enjoy a nice ride like the ones you've given me. It wouldn't be fair for me to be selfish, would it? Share and share alike, my granny

213

always told me, and who am I to ignore the wisdom of my elders?'

I had earlier wondered if Meg was having a physical relationship with the giant Scandinavian, but now I realised she clearly could not have been, for the look of amazement that froze her face as she felt him beginning to enter her was no act. She turned her head to glance at him over her shoulder, desperately trying to get a glimpse of the fearful weapon that was about to take her.

'No, please!' she shrieked, to my utter astonishment, for I had not expected her to beg for mercy. 'Please, no!' she wailed as the head of Erik's cock began stretching her entrance. 'I'll give you money, clothes, horses, anything, just don't, please!'

'Too late,' I growled, and slapped Erik's rump.

He gave an involuntary jerk forward and buried four to five inches of his erection inside her.

'Right in,' I urged, and he obliged. 'Yes, he's a big bastard, isn't he Megan?' I grabbed her hair and lifted her head. 'And he can keep this up for a very long time, believe me I know, and soon you will too.'

'No,' she wailed as I released my grip on her hair and Erik pulled back to thrust forward again. Then for a moment he just stood there buried deep inside her, his arms tied helplessly behind his back.

I smiled up at him. 'Either you fuck her properly,' I said menacingly, 'or I'll take a whip to your arse and you'll fuck her anyway. Then I'll take the same whip to her arse when you're through with her.'

He saw there was nothing for it and began pumping in and out of Meg in that languid, steady rhythm I knew so well. She tried to resist, grinding her teeth and biting her lip until it nearly bled, but there are some things in nature that cannot be controlled, and not all storms happen on the outside.

After about ten minutes, Meg succumbed to the steady pounding between her legs and climaxed, shrieking a torrent of abuse while laughing like a maniac, after which she stopped fighting the experience completely. Like me as Angelina, she discovered just how many times it's possible for a woman to come when the man has the staying power of a steam engine and the self-control of a monk, and especially when he is under direct orders not to orgasm himself until given permission to do so.

Eventually, however, I relented, for by now Meg was becoming exhausted. Although her body still shook beneath involuntary spasms of pleasure, her head hung motionless and her arms and legs seemed to have gone limp.

'Okay, Erik,' I said, 'let it rip, and make it a good one!'

And he made it a good one, all right. With a sudden roar, he threw his head back and arched his spine as he climaxed.

Despite her exhausted state, Meg raised her head and groaned as his orgasm filled her to bursting. 'You... you bitch!' she wailed, her red-rimmed eyes staring wildly up at me. 'You absolute little bitch! I'll kill you for this, I swear it!'

'Yes, well, you can try,' I retorted, 'but right now I'm the one calling the shots here, so I'd say you were well and truly fucked, lady.'

'That was awful,' I said. 'I'm sorry. I shouldn't have done all that in there. I don't know what came over me.'

'She deserved everything she got.' Andy patted my arm

with his soft little brown hand. I still hadn't quite come to terms with the fact that it was my Andy inside that pretty little body and that the breasts I could see through the slightly gaping top of her dress were real now and not padding, as when he was playing Andrea.

We were standing in the last room at the end of the stone building, having left our prisoners next door, Meg still bound over the frame and Erik with his manacled wrists leashed to one of the wall rings originally installed for my benefit.

'It was still wrong, though,' I sighed. 'She was terrified and now she's lost the plot altogether, I reckon.'

'Well, maybe she'll think twice before she does the same thing to someone else in the future,' Andy retorted, 'though I shouldn't hold my breath, if I were you. There's something about her that is really evil.'

'I know,' I agreed. 'It's like an aura, though you can't actually see it.'

'Well, the sooner we get as far away from her as possible, the better, and I've been thinking about that and about your little plan. I don't reckon I should bring Meg up anywhere near the house. She's mental enough to try something silly, and if this gun goes bang up there, we'll have the lot of them down on our heads.'

'Well, you can't stay here with her, Andy. Once we get the carriage sorted out we'll need to get going straightaway, before someone hears us. Those things aren't exactly quiet, you know, and horses make a lot of noise all by themselves.'

'No, I shan't stay here,' he said, 'but *she* will, only we won't let Erik know that. You and he will go on ahead and let him think I'm bringing the bitch along just close enough so I can make sure everything's going smoothly. If you can grab one of the maids, and get everything sorted on the food and clothes front, I'll do a quick scout of the stables and make sure the coast is clear, but I'll keep out of sight until everything is hitched up and ready to go.'

'And we just leave Megan here?' I asked uncertainly.

He nodded. 'We take Erik along, but Megan stays here. It might just win us a bit of extra time, especially if she takes your place.'

'My place?' I echoed. 'How do you mean?'

'Well, she's a bit bigger than you, but I reckon that doggie suit thing will fit her well enough, and on all fours she won't look as tall as she is. We do her up as if she were you, complete with the gag thing, and let her stay here. If anyone comes looking for her in the morning, they'll find the doggie girl they expect to see and assume Erik is somewhere about his business. And if we're really lucky, they may not realise the carriage is gone. If someone does realise it's missing and Erik's not about the place, they might assume he's taken it to go somewhere on one of Meg's errands.'

'Maybe,' I said dubiously, 'but they'll realise the truth soon enough.'

'Not soon enough for us not to be twenty or thirty miles up the road from here.'

'But where are we going to go?'

Andy shrugged. 'Who cares? Anywhere has got to be an improvement over this place, although I must say, this is a very cute body.' He giggled.

I shook my head. Some things never changed.

'Anyway,' he went on seriously, 'once we get in the

clear we can stop and think properly. Right now, we don't know how long we're going to stay like this, so the sooner we get out of here, the better for Angelina and Indira when they get their bodies back again.'

'Okay,' I relented. His plan made sense. It was unlikely that Angelina would act and react like me, and Indira, even though she was apparently capable of killing, was not Andy, with his surprisingly quick wit and the total irreverence which was his best weapon in adversity. 'Yes,' I said with more confidence, turning back towards the door, 'let's do it your way.'

And so it was that less than an hour later a new bitch dog took up her residence in my former kennel, and it was obvious that she was no more enamoured of the situation than I had been.

She stood on all fours, her discomfort registering plainly on her face, for not only was the leather dog suit tight on her but I had made sure Erik laced it as cruelly as possible. Now he waited to fit the gag, but Meg was determined to have one last word.

'I'll find you no matter how far you run!' she cried. 'I'll find you, Angelina, and I'll make this look like a child's nursery game when I do.' Her eyes glared madly up at me, fury at her helplessness making them gleam brightly in the lantern light.

I laughed and patted her on the head, wondering if I shouldn't have Erik shave her hair as he had been instructed to shave mine. 'Down, Fido,' I said. 'Be a good doggie or I'll have Uncle Erik here give you another bone.' I nodded to Erik, who moved forward to press the steel gag mechanism into place. He then held up the padded dog mask. 'Quite an ugly bitch, really,' I murmured. 'Say woof, there's a good girl.'

Outside in the darkness, Erik stood a little ways from us holding a lantern. He was just far enough away that he couldn't hear us talking, but not so far away that he would risk doing anything stupid. Besides, with Andy holding the pistol, and me gripping the knife, and mad Meg now helpless and silent, he had little option but to go along with us.

'Just watch yourself,' Andy whispered. 'I'll be close by, but in the house you'll be on your own, so don't take any risks.'

'You neither,' I urged. 'Keep well back, and if it comes to it, run like hell. One of us has to stay free, whatever happens.'

'We'll see,' he said. 'I wouldn't leave you, not now, not after what we've just done to her.' He jerked a thumb back to indicate the blockhouse. 'She's gonna be madder than hell. I reckon it would be kinder to shoot you than let you fall into her clutches again.'

'Yes, I reckon you could be right,' I muttered grimly. I looked towards Erik, who was standing with his back to us. 'Ready?' I whispered.

Beside me, Andy took my hand and squeezed it. 'Yep,' he said. 'Let's see what the past has in store for us now, shall we?'

Epilogue

And there, dear reader, the story must end – this part of the story, at least. I should like to describe to you how we managed to get clothing, money, food and another pistol from the house, and tell you about our flight in the carriage past the gate as we clattered away into the night. Unfortunately, I don't know any of the details myself, for we were only halfway to the house when I suddenly found myself back at Anne-Marie's place, still astride Andy and very close to coming.

Andy beat me to it but it was a reflex action; he came out of his own trance as the tremors faded. He lay there for several long seconds, bemused and stunned, trying to come to terms with what had happened and with the fact that he had now experienced the same incredible phenomenon I had. We lay together and talked about it for hours, and then, when the sun had driven away the morning mists, we woke Anne-Marie and related our story to her.

We were to go back in time again shortly, together once more, but by the time we arrived in our borrowed bodies our coach was already well on the road to London, with Erik up on the driver's bench. We could have asked him how things had gone, of course, but then that would have given our game away completely and neither of us felt so wise, not at that point.

It was not to be the last we saw of Mad Megan

Crowthorne or her supposed master, Gregory Hacklebury, for I had awakened in her a dreadful need to be avenged and she was not a woman to take an insult like that lying down – on all fours as a doggie girl, yes, but not lying down, not once she was free again to do something about the indignities I had made her suffer.

But all that will have to wait, at least for the moment, as the adventures that followed our nocturnal carriage ride are enough to fill at least one more volume.

Did we finally solve the mystery of Great Marlins and the apparent disappearance from the scene of Meg and Greg? Well, that's for me to know and for you to wait to find out, I'm afraid, for it is now close to bedtime and tomorrow I have a very important appointment with Bill... Bill Shakespeare, that is. I've promised to help him with a plotline that's giving him a bit of trouble, and it's either me or that dreadful Bacon fellow who's a terrible bore, farts a lot, and insists on making much ado about nothing. And, oh yes, he also keeps staring at my breasts, which I think you'll agree is very rude of him and not at all the behaviour of a fellow some scholars still try to insist was the real bard. If you ask me, Bacon couldn't write his way out of a paper bag and Bill should put him on his bike once and for all. Not that he ever listens to my advice, mind you, but we live in hope.

So, it's goodbye for the present everyone and much love now, in the future and in the past,

Teena xx

More exciting titles available from Chimera

* * *